IMAGINE CADE

BRANDED

JD GOLD

outskirts
press

Imagine Cade
Branded
All Rights Reserved.
Copyright © 2019 JD Gold
v2.0

This is a work of fiction. The events and characters described herein are imaginary and are not intended to refer to specific places or living persons. The opinions expressed in this manuscript are solely the opinions of the author and do not represent the opinions or thoughts of the publisher. The author has represented and warranted full ownership and/or legal right to publish all the materials in this book.

This book may not be reproduced, transmitted, or stored in whole or in part by any means, including graphic, electronic, or mechanical without the express written consent of the publisher except in the case of brief quotations embodied in critical articles and reviews.

Outskirts Press, Inc.
http://www.outskirtspress.com

ISBN: 978-1-4787-3736-0

Cover Photo © 2019 gettyimages.com. All rights reserved - used with permission.

Outskirts Press and the "OP" logo are trademarks belonging to Outskirts Press, Inc.

PRINTED IN THE UNITED STATES OF AMERICA

Dedicated to danni/posty and samurai/marvel

Chapter 1

I woke up earlier than usual on a Tuesday morning. I had the strangest dream, and I couldn't fall back to sleep. I did my usual routine: get out of bed, get dressed, brush my teeth, put on makeup (only a little bit because my mother goes insane if I have too much), pack my bag, and eat breakfast. My mother was on the phone as I was eating honey nut cheerios that I'm pretty sure were stale. As I was eating my last bite of cereal, I could hear her say, "You can always reach me if you need anything. We all need help at times like these, I am here for you." She came into the dining room, her eyes filled with tears, struggling to hold them back. I asked if everything was alright. She didn't speak, but sat me down on our black leather couch, and held my hand. Her hands were cold, and severely shaking.

"I just got off the phone with Cade's mother..."
"Is everything okay?"
"Cade is..."
"What mom, is everything okay? What? Tell me please."
She took a deep breath in and slowly exhaled.
"Cade is dead."
"What on earth are you talking about? I just saw her at school yesterday and I was texting her all night."
"She was reported missing at 11 o'clock last night, sweetie.
I could feel the sadness and confusion bottling up inside of me.
"This can't be true. W-why.. W-who.. How did this happen?"

"She snuck out last night to go see her boyfriend, Cameron."

"So she's at Camerons... Not missing?"

At this moment, I could barely speak.

"They called Cameron... She never showed up at his place. A body was found that fit her description,. I am *so* sorry honey."

Tears came streaming down my face and my vision was blurred. I buried my head in my mom's lap rocking back and forth, sobbing uncontrollably. My cheeks were stained with an endless river of tears, as I was enduring the emotional pain that continued to swallow me up. I wish I could crawl back into my nightmare, It was better than this.

Mom said I didn't need to go to school. But I thought I should. Cade would want me to see Cameron and Ash and go to school . So I went to school and prepared for the rest of my life.

It had been a couple of days since the funeral. My heart was empty. I had no reason to believe Cade was alive, and that reason took me down. I had cried for hours without eating. My mom lay with me and that was comforting, but the fact Cade was dead sent shockwaves to my heart.

The bus ride to school was a blur. Painful and surreal. I didn't have Cade laughing across from me, telling jokes about how life at home with her brother was so awful. Here and there an argument had occurred in my family with my mom or siblings, and Cade was the only one to see my side. She saw the "rebel within me," and sometimes Cade made fun of me for that. I don't want to feel like I am the bad guy, I just have a big mind and apparently mouth, as Cade says. I don't know what I was going to do without her. This was not supposed to happen.

I arrived at school late, so I had to rush to my first class, biology. Sitting next to me was supposed to be Cade; looking at the empty seat, made me feel as though my soul had vaporized.

During attendance, the teacher looked at me as she called out "Cade Murphy." I looked down at my lap, doing my best to hold back the tears that were dripping down my cheek. I was lost in my thoughts when I heard the loudspeaker in the school with the principal repeating the words, "Good morning, RidgeHill, As you know our very own student Cade Murphy has passed away. This is a loss for all of us, I am sorry for you all." I tilted my head up from the floor and looked back to her seat, and sitting there was Cade. I looked at her, trying to scan her body for any damage. She was saying something, but I couldn't hear anything that came from her mouth. Something grabbed me from behind and I jumped in surprise. Cameron, Cade's boyfriend, turned me around and asked if I was okay.

"Yeah, sure."

I looked at the direction of Cade's seat, but there was nothing there, only an empty seat with a lost soul. I was incredulous as I was unable to believe what had just happened. As I sat down, I heard a whisper from my right. I looked, and sitting there was Cade -- again. There was a hushing sound coming out of her mouth, but no words to complete the expressions on her face. "What?" I said. "What are you saying?" The whole class looked at me.

"Nick, what are you doing?" Cameron said with a baffled look on his face, touching my shoulder. I haven't heard that name since the last time I saw Cade. That was like our signal when something was wrong and only since last year we let Cameron in on in it so I guess it just made me feel uncomfortable because I imagined Cade's voice saying that.

"I can see Cade."

"I think you should go to the nurse, Nick."

"How do you not see her? She's right there?" I looked back at Cameron who looked in the seat. His eyes grew bigger and his face somehow became a strangers.

"Nick….."

"But- Cade. She is right there." I looked at Cade who was looking straight forward at the board hissing a sound.

"Sit down, Nikki!" The teacher scolded. How did they not see her? Clearly, Cade was there, with her blonde hair in a ponytail sitting silently. Cameron grabbed my arms and took out his phone.

"Ash, get in here now." Cameron said.

I started crying and dropped my head into Cameron's shoulder. His voice strained as he comforted me by rubbing my hair.

"I know, I miss her too." Cameron whispered in my ear. I was losing my mind and I didn't know what to do. I was shaken from seeing Cade's body right next to me. Whether to think it was a dream or some type of illusion- I wouldn't know, until later.

Within minutes, Ash ran into the room and skidded to the ground. "Nikki." Ash walked into the room. Cameron let go of me and was replaced by Ash when his cologne, ax, suffocated my nose and slowed my breath down.

"She is going through a lot, give her some slack." He said to the teacher. I could hear Ash swearing under his breath.

"Ash, watch your behavior!" The teacher raised her voice and stamped her foot on the floor.

"Yeh? What are you going to do? All you do is yell." Ash said. He put his hands through his soft hair and took my arm.

"Let's go."

"Where are we going?" I asked sniffling.

"Where are you going Mr. Gallen?" The teacher crossed her arms and looked sternly at Ash and me.

"Anywhere, but here." He whispered in my ear. "Hastalavista." I laughed forcely, but half of it was because Ash was just so inappropriate which made me love him even more. I wiped my eyes and started walking out of the classroom.

"I will text you." I heard Cameron say. I didn't have the energy to respond back so I continued moving.

"Come back here!" The teacher yelled, but we were already out the door running to Ash's motorcycle. Ash is old for a sophomore; he's 17, and is allowed to drive his vehicle anywhere. Sometimes when I am feeling down, we would sneak out and go on midnight drives. We met over the summer going into freshman year, I was surprised he fell for me, but obviously he saw what other guys didn't. When I told him I didn't have a boyfriend, he seemed shocked. I guess I wasn't confident in myself to think that a boy would like me. But seriously, although I can be a handful and love doing things that make my life feel thrilling, guys weren't my best forte. That has all changed in high school. Although nothing serious has happened between us yet, I'm anxious to get to that part in our relationship. I'm a 16 year old mature girl, who knows my limits.

"Are you ready, Nick?" That's another thing; Ash calls me that too, but usually when he needs to say something important.

"Go." I laughed and crossed my arms around his waist.

The motor engine got my heart beating louder and the helmet on Ash's face made me smile. I could see the sweat dripping from the sides of his ears and I wanted to wipe them away, but he looked so hot with it. I squeezed my arms around his waist and lay my head on his shoulder. Let the wind take me away; I could fall free now. There was nothing holding me back.

We finally stopped in front of a mountain glowing with city lights. I looked at Ash and gave him one of those "I can't believe you did this" expressions.

"What? I know you love this, so shut up and drink." He tossed me a can of diet coke and I popped the cap off. The sparkling coke satisfied my thirst and created a bubble in my nose. Ash looked at me and I started coughing. "God Nikki, why do I love you?"

I walked up to him where he was sitting on the ground looking forward.

"I don't know, why do you?" I laughed and he leaned in and our lips touched. When I was a younger, I used to be so scared of kissing guys so I would practice on a glass. My mother told me it would just come naturally, and she was right. Ash told me the first time we kissed that I was actually really good.

"Stand up." He took my hands and pulled me up.

"For what?" I looked into his greenish-brown eyes.

"Do you trust me? Now, close your eyes." Ash moved in the back of me and grabbed the side of my hips. I closed my eyes slowly to mark off where I was last. I could feel his breath near my ear and his grip on my waist. He continued walking me until I felt the edge no land in front of me. "Ash." I said scared.

"Look."

I opened my eyes and there was a huge drop, but in front of me was the beautiful city. I had an idea, but I didn't know if it was crazy or stupid. "Hold my hands," I said.

"What are you doing?" He asked.

"Do you trust me?"

Ash smiled. I walked forward and tilted against the mountain. "Nikki." Ash's voice lifted.

"Just hold me." His grip almost crushed my hand, but it didn't matter because I felt free. I was falling towards the bottom ready to see what was going to happen, but something was holding me back. The dream repeated in my mind as I tried to remember every piece of it. Slowing my breath, I ignored it for now and felt the cold wind blowing in my face. I leaned more and could feel me losing the grip of Ash, but I didn't care. I took a deep breathe with my eyes closed and breathed out "Ahhhhhhhhhh." In that moment I felt like nothing could stop me. Like I was unbeatable. But I knew that feeling wouldn't last for long as my best friend was dead. I laughed and backed my feet up onto the cliff. "You are crazy Nick." I was about to respond. "But I don't care." Ash touched the side of my cheek as he knows I hate when people touch my hair. He's probably the only person I let do it. "Let's go back before your mom kills me."

Chapter 2

Ash and I went out for something to eat on the way back to my house. He walked me to my doorstep as usual and kissed me goodnight. My mother was sitting there waiting for me as I walked inside.

"Goodnight Ms. Field!" Ash shouted as I stepped in the door.

"You can call me Susan, Ash."

"Whatever floats your boat, Ms. Field." He smiled that smile I fell for over the summer.

"Goodbye, Ash. Your mother is probably wondering where you are."

"Yeah, yeah. I'll see you tomorrow, Nick. If you are having any problems, I'm just a phone call away."

"Thanks Ash, Night."

Ash started up his motorcycle, I could hear the engine roar. It was 10 o'clock and I was getting ready to go to bed. What a day.

After brushing my teeth and putting on my favorite pajamas, ones with wolves on them, I switched the bedside lamp off and threw myself under the covers. About 10 minutes into trying to sleep, my position kept bothering me so I moved more than I was used to. My neck began to hurt and my frustration started to kick in, but I knew what to do.

I picked up my phone and dialed Ash. "Thought you would never call." He said sarcastically.

"Shut up, can't you just read my mind?" I could sense a grin on his face.

"Nick, I would dream of doing that, but then where would be the fun fighting for you?"

Right now I could imagine talking to Cade about problems with life; including Ash. Our relationship is up and down and we love each other so much that's why it's so hard. We both love to do dangerous things and take risks. Our love sometimes backfires on us. I haven't cheated on him nor has he on me, but sometimes he can get busy with football. At least Ash knew how much I needed him now.

We continued talking on the phone 'till 2am until my mom came in to check on me.

"Hi sweetie, I know you are talking with Ash, but can you try falling asleep?" I took a deep breath and considered there were worse problems in the world.

"Got to go, Ash." I turned my body toward my bedside table.

"Night Nick, love you."

"Love you too." I whispered so that my mom couldn't hear. I ended the phone call and turned off my phone so no other distractions could get in my way.

"Thanks, honey. If you need me I will be in my room." she closed the door slightly. I yawned and tried to make myself comfortable as I didn't know what I would be in for tonight.

I was being lured into a black hole. A man with sharp teeth, like a vampire and ice skin gently touching my hands. He kept telling me I was safe and alright. I thought I knew him from somewhere, so I followed him and got myself into a mess. He closed the door on me. I turned around to see deformed faces. I knew then, death was talking to me. And darkness was calling for me.

I heard Cade's voice disappear ending with the word "me." It was a dream, that I simply thanked God wasn't real. At least I hoped it wasn't real.

I picked up the phone and contacted Cameron. Scrolling down I saw Cade's number and pressed on the screen, calling it. Pretending to hear the voice of Cade, I discarded the voicemail and just talked to her normally. "Hey girl, where have you been? Cameron is missing you and Ash took me on this amazing ride. It was pretty cool. We should hango-." Before I finished the sentence my mother came in the door.

"Nick, Who are you talking to?" I paused for a second thinking about my lame response that I was going to say.

"Just a friend." I waited until mother closed the door to realize I was not going to do that again. I clicked on Cameron's number, ringing with agony to spill my dream.

"Uh, hello? Nick?" His voice strained and yawned from the time of day it was.

"Sorry, but I need to tell you something. It's about Cade."

"What? What's happened?" He coughed to get his high pitched voice straightened out.

"Well....." trying to think if I was going to disappoint him. "It was a dream."

He scoffed. "Nikki, I thought you were gonna say you got a message or something."

"Well it was kind of like that, but she's dead, we know that." Rushing to finish the sentence before he managed to hang-up on me. "I think she is in danger."

"What do you mean?" He asked. Now I was thinking that there was no point in making Cameron feel worse about Cade.

"She was hurt in my dream, like she was calling for help, *literally*."

"It's probably just getting to you, I get it, but it's going to be okay." He responded.

I sighed and ended the call because I could tell he wasn't going to believe me. This was a sign, I knew it had to be. There was a way Cade was calling my name. Dreams can seem so real, but this was like I was there with her; watching Cade suffer from whatever she was going through. She isn't dead. No. She isn't, but what now? I figured to start from where this all happened and see if I could communicate with her. I was going to find my best friend and prove to everyone she was alive. At least, right now she is.

I barely slept the whole night, just thinking about school. I had brushed my teeth and picked out an okay outfit that didn't make me look sloppy or like I cared. "Honey," my mom said in her sweet attentive voice, "have a good breakfast before Ash picks you up."

"How do you know he is picking me up?"

"Called the house this morning."

I walked into the kitchen where my mom was cooking up eggs and a blended smoothie. I sat on the chair that I could spin in, which was one of my favorite parts of the house, besides my room. Escape was a big thing for me these days. I had begged my mom to get a motorcycle of some sort for me, but all she kept blabbering about was how they were dangerous. I didn't really care. I loved riding with Ash, but I wanted one of my own where I could just go out whenever. Though, my room was kind of like that. I had made some sort of fort on one side of my bed. At night, I would take a flashlight, book and read with what felt like a guard around me. Mom had barged in a couple of times, but that didn't stop me from doing what I loved most.

I ate my breakfast and put my helmet on. Ash got it for me last year for my birthday. It was black and had graffiti on the sides. The inside was coated in elms fur that kept my head and ears warm from the cold weather. However, sometimes when I was totally out of my mind, I would take it off along with my jacket and just hold on tight to Ash for my life. After, I would wrap a blanket around myself and think about the rush I just felt. Thankfully, that didn't die when Cade did.

I heard a honk from the driveway and assumed it was Ash. As soon as I got out a cop was standing next to Ash with something in his hands. I unbuckled the helmet and scooped it up in my hands walking towards both of them. "Everything okay officer?" I looked at the object which was pink; he softly laid the shirt on my hands. I opened it and read the words SWEET. I knew what it was, Cade's shirt. When we went on school trips together we bought something every time. The time we went to disneyland we bought a couple shirt that said "sweet and sour." I'm sorry, Miss."

"Where did you find it?" I asked.

"Down by the park, it was on the grass."

"Why are you giving it to me? Don't you need it for evidence or something?"

"Yes, however, I wanted to ask you if this was Cade's. "

"Yeah." I forced a smile. The officer nodded and went back into his car.

"Well sorry Nick, but now that that's over with, can we go?" Ash said with an uncomfortable laugh.

"Shut up." I punched him on the shoulder with my fist and gave him a kiss on the cheek. The engine rumbled and the sound was music to my ears. "Before we go to school, can we stop by the park?"

"Really, Nikki?" Ash said surprised, but not annoyed.

"Yeah, now go." I said with no hesitation.

We stopped right in front of the park. Ash had waited on the bike and parked in a spot while I did what I came here to do, which was find answers. I didn't run, but didn't take my time getting there. I knew where it was because of the yellow tape that crossed around the tree saying "do not cross." I scanned the ground where I saw some red grass, my body tingled. I looked and walked around the circle seeing if a sign would show me what to do, but I got nothing. I took a deep breathe. *Cade if you can hear me, where are you, how do I find you? Are you alive?* I waited about two minutes not flinching and listening to the things around me. "Nick, come on!" I heard Ash shout from his motor. I walked away feeling hopeless and upset.

"But I saw..." I turned back and saw Cade lying near the tree. She was rocking back and forth looking straight forward. "Cade! How is this happening? Where are you?" I wanted her to look at me. I yelled throwing up my hands, but she made no movement.

A few seconds later, Cade managed to shift her head slightly. I walked under the rope and called out to Ash telling him I would be there shortly. I got as close as I thought was reasonable and looked Cade straight in the eyes. "Nick, I'm alive," she whispered.

Chapter 3

Those words. They were everything, more than anything would ever mean to me; to my whole life. A feeling inside me made my life feel unrealistic all of the sudden.

I started following Cade who was running in front me, chasing, like she had a destination. She kept looking back with her scared smile, and eyes that sizzled like someone was following her. I tried catching up to Cade and kept yelling her name to the point where Cade faded in the distance. I was a few feet in front of the bike staring into the distance.

"Nick, are you ok?"

"I saw her," still looking straight.

"Cade?" He asked.

I tried to meet his eyes, slowly lifting them. "Yeah."

"What do you mean?"

"She….. is, alive." My eyes opened.

"Alright babe, stop playing games."

"No, no, I swear Ash… I saw her and she told me tha-"

"Okay, I know you are upset, but this isn't funny, just hop on or we're going to be late."

"Why don't you believe me?" I said angrily.

"Babe-"

"You know what? I'll just walk."

"Seriously?"

I crossed my arms. "Suit yourself." Ash sped off on his

bike, the fastest I've ever seen him go. I picked up my bag and began to walk.

As I made my way, I started daydreaming. The world became a blur and reality was no longer there. The memories of Cade came flooding back and I felt my legs go numb. I fell to the ground but there was something wrong. I couldn't stop falling. I was in a hole of thoughts and flashbacks. I could hear Cade's voice calling me and could see small images of us when we were younger. As reality started flooding back in, I had to get out of here.

By the time I arrived at school, I had missed the first two periods; Math and Spanish. Turned out we had a pop-quiz in Spanish so I got a big fat zero for missing it; I tried arguing my point, but it was useless. It was around 10:25 when I heard my name being called to the principal's office over the loudspeaker. Being the childish teenagers they were, all the boys went "Oooooooh" and stared at me as my face turned red. I picked up my bag and made my way to the office. I was seated in a red and black chair as I waited for Mr. Berkins to come into his office. The door opened and my mom and Mr. Berkins, and the Vice principal, Ms. Shallick, walked in. My mom rushed over to me and looked me straight in the eye and asked if I was okay.

"Yes, mom. I'm fine."

"Wasn't Ash supposed to bring you in? Why were you so late?"

"We sort of got in a fight and I said I would walk."

"Now why would yo-" She was interrupted by Mr. Berkins who then took charge of the situation.

"Now Ms. Field, let's just calm down and assess the

situation. Thank you Ms. Shalleck." She exited the room. The principal had crossed his fingers and lay them on his desk. I looked at my mom and her mouth was closed shut.

"I'm sorry, I didn't want to ride with him," I said innocently.

"What did Ash do?" My mom spoke.

I was thinking about what I was going to say. I didn't want to sound like a freak, but I saw what I saw. I bit my lip hoping someone would ask a new question. "Honey?"

I looked at her, then the teacher and then back down at my pants. "Um, well, you are not going to believe me, so I probably shouldn't. Just give me a punishment."

"Nick, we are not going to punish you."

Mrs. Berkins cleared her throat and my mom looked at her.

"Sorry, *I* won't punish you."

"I.. I saw Cade." I didn't look up.

"Honey, she's dead."

I got up from the chair and looked at her. "I saw what I saw! I knew you weren't going to believe me. Just stop, I don't care." I turned around and ran straight for the outside door. I know what I needed to do: find Cameron. I ran to the front of the school and saw him through the window sitting in the back of the classroom. I texted him.

Me: Look to the window

He put away his phone and our eyes met. "What are you doing out there?" He mouthed. I looked down, around, then back up; my phone buzzed.

Cameron: I'm coming out

I lowered my hand and saw Cameron leave the classroom trying to force his feet to run. About 30 seconds later,

I felt a hand slip on and off my shoulder so I turned around. "Cameron, I need to show you something."

"What?"

"Please?"

"You're scaring me Nick."

"Please, It's important."

"I have class."

"Just come." I interlocked his hands into mine and pulled him running. Cameron looked back into the class and caught the teacher's attention.

"There's no going back." He ran for it and I followed him. I let go of his hand and led the way back to the park. I was running, no distractions, no time. People were looking for me and eventually would for Cameron. But, this was more important. Way, more.

The whole way we were silent with Cameron following my tracks and trying to comprehend what was happening and where we were going.

Running was the only option at this point. There was no time to waste. About five minutes later we arrived on the green field. He spoke, "Why are we here?"

I walked forward to the tree and stopped. Turned around to Cameron, "I saw her."

"Cade?"

"Yes." We still looked at each other, but his expression changed. I was the one who felt crazy in my own mind, but what I should be doing is trusting it. I took a deep breath. "I'll prove it."

"Let's go, this isn't funny."

"Let me do it."

"Fine. Ok, go ahead."

I turned around and looked at the tree, then at the entire green field. It didn't feel empty like it was. Cade was with me here. I felt it. I felt her. It's not easy to describe how I know. I mean, yes, she is communicating with me, but it's more than that. It's like a string in my heart hooked onto both ends and I could feel it connected. It hasn't stopped which means Cade's alive. I looked at the tree. "Cade, I know you can hear me." I heard a voice mumbling something. "Cade, listen to me, answer me!" My tone raised.

"Nick." She spooked me. I turned. "Help." Cade pushed forward her arm with red bruises and pressed down on them.

"Nikki, who are you talking to?" Cameron backed away.

"Cade, tell me something about Cameron I don't know."

"You're crazy Nick." He rolled his eyes; I looked back at Cade.

She looked up from her bruises to me. "He shouldn't be here." Then cocked her head towards Cameron. "He had a secret crush on you in eighth grade."

I looked at Cameron with shock. "What?" he asked.

"Cade says, that you had a crush on me..... In the beginning of eighth grade."

His face turned red and shock grew on his face. "No, you probably knew that."

"I didn't, I promise."

"Tell me something else, I don't believe you."

Cade interrupted. " He told me he loved me when I was sleeping and thought I didn't hear it."

I looked at her, then to Cameron. My eyes were about to tear from the look on Cade's face. Hopelessness with insight, Distraught with purpose, Anger with reason.

"Nikki, what's wrong?" He came closer to me, I backed away. "The first time you told Cade you loved her, she was sleeping."

"What?! I told her not to tell anyone." Cameron turned slowly the other way.

My voice was going to grow stronger. "I told you. She didn't tell me." I said, firm as hell.

"How is this possible?" Cameron put his hands over his head.

"I don't know. I don't know." But maybe that's okay. When you really think about it- it's an oxymoron. We are lost in time trying to figure out the answer. But life is undefined. There is no solution. I still hoped there was solution for this problem.

"Cade where are you?" I asked. She kept moving farther. "Stop, where are you going?"

"He's coming!" Cade looked behind her.

"Who?"

"It's dark, small."

"Who is coming Cade?" She kept walking farther and faster.

"Nick, find me." With that she disappeared and there was no trace of her.

What was I going to do now? She could be anywhere. "Nick?"

"Yeah?" I turned around to Cameron.

"How can you see her?... Can you see ghosts?"

The question hit me hard. I never really thought why I could see Cade, and if I could communicate with anyone else. Was I given some kind of gift? I don't know if it felt like one, but if it was going to help me find my friend, then please, do it fast.

"I.. I don't know."

"what did she say?"

"She is somewhere dark, small. And it's a guy who took her." A tear started dropping from my eye, and I couldn't help but lean into Cameron. He caught me faintly and my head rested on his strong chest.

"We will find her," he said, his voice confident.

"I hope we will." I realized the dream that I had was a warning and symbol something went wrong. That was that mark that led me to believing she was alive.

I looked up to see a rainbow above our heads. Perfect timing. pink, blue and red. Pink for possible, blue for believing, red for revenge. Yellow, orange, green. Yellow for yelling. Orange for optimistic, green for good. It's possible I'm believing in revenge. I'm yelling for optimism to be good. But right now nothing seems possible. There's no pink, blue, orange, or green. Only red and yellow completing my rainbow.

Chapter 4

I heard a sound on the window. I got up from my bed and put on a sweatshirt. Walking towards the window, I saw rocks being thrown at the glass. I opened it and saw Cameron in all black with his tiny flashlight directing it straight into my eyes; I grabbed my phone.

Me: What are you doing??

Cameron: Come down now

Cameron: !

Without replying back, I grabbed a sweatshirt and closed my door softly. My parent's room was across from mine, so I walked carefully making sure I was quiet. Walking quietly was one of my weaknesses, I would stomp my feet on the carpet walking up and down the stairs.

I opened the door and locked it from the outside. Cameron ran over to me with a confused expression on his face. "Why are you getting me so late?"

"Cause we are going to find Cade." Cameron said.

"What? How? Why now?" Cameron must be crazy to think we could do it right now. With whose help? It was funny because Cameron was so against me in the beginning and now he's the one convincing me.

"We need to get Cade's phone, it might have something that we can use."

I followed Cameron and turned on my flashlight. The wind blew in my face causing the coldness to touch upon my nose. Cameron turned the car on and I opened the door to the front seat.

"Do you know where to go?" I asked looking at my phone. "It could be anywhere at the station." The engine made a rough sound as he slowly stepped on the gas pedal.

"I got the key from my mom." The car started to move and I looked at my phone. "What is it?" Cameron asked.

Ash was calling me, but why? We haven't talked in days and I don't understand what he could possibly want or need at this hour. "Ash is calling me." I looked at Cameron to see his response. His eyes narrowed and his jaw lined tightened. I didn't know what to say to that, so I looked back at my phone and answered it. "Hi." I didn't let myself go soft.

"Nikki, where are you?"

"Why do you care?"

"Your mom is calling me, going crazy. She came to check on you and you weren't there. She tried calling you, but there was no signal."

I looked to Cameron and held my hand over the phone. "My mom knows I'm not there." I placed the phone back again to my ear. "Please cover for me!" I was disappointed Ash was only calling about that, but it was good to hear his voice.

"Ok, I will."

"Thanks Ash."

"And.-"

I interrupted him before he had time to speak.

"What?"

"Nothing, Bye Nick." By saying Nick, it maybe meant he felt bad and wanted us to be an *us* again. I didn't have anything to be sorry for.

"What did he say?" Cameron asked.

"He said he would." I turned off my phone and slipped it into my pocket.

We pulled into the driveway of the station and turned off the lights of the car.

"Take this flashlight." He reached his hand out to the back of the car and pulled out a big yellow light. Handing it to me, I closed the door and started walking to the front of the building. I hope this would work and Cameron and I could find some sort of clue. Just anything to help us direct where to go next.

Cameron caught up with me and went in front to put the key in. Waiting for it to click or turn was more nerve wracking than I thought, but when it went off, I sighed of relief. "Come on." I looked back at Cameron and then to the black hallway. I switched on the flashlight and aimed it around me. Coming to the front of a desk with filed papers , I saw a tag that mentioned the name Chief Jones.

"Where do we go?" I looked at Cameron who was in the room across looking through the draws. He huffed and dug through the files to find the phone. His face told me how he was feeling: frustrated. He came to the last draw and I heard a plastic sound pop open in the background.

"Got it." Cameron said while taking out the black iphone. From a distance the stain of red streak marks twisted my stomach, and me. I swiftly ran over to him and grabbed the phone pressing on the home button. I looked through her messages; ones from family and Cameron, then me. The last thing I had said to her: "be careful, love you."

A tear dropped from eye and I lost my heart into the words

of the text. I sniffed and wiped my face. I didn't look up to see Cameron and the intensity of his guilt. I wanted to be mad at him, at the same time I couldn't. *Ugh, so cheesy Nikki. Get a hold of yourself. I'm gonna find her, I'm gonna find you Cade. I promise.* Unexpectedly, a message popped on the phone and my heart skipped a beat. I went into the app where it came from and saw the message.

Hey, Do you need some tutoring?
What? What is this?
My fingers typed.
I responded.
Leave me the hell alone.

I nudged Cameron and felt his body lean in closer to the screen. I looked at him and his eyes widened. We both waited.

Boy, I was just asking. You liked when I helped you last time.

I didn't understand this, tutoring? For what, Cade? I was the one always asking her questions about homework. She would finish her tests or quizzes before everyone else. It wasn't necessarily a bad thing, that's just the way Cade worked. Why would she need a tutor? This site looked suspicious as I was scrolling down the names of the people she had contact with.

Cameron grabbed the phone from me and scrolled to another message I seemed to miss. I read over his shoulder the words.

I can help you in person- where would you like to meet?

I felt Cameron's body shiver; like a twitch that caused my body to react with my head sinking onto his shoulder. I whispered, "scroll up," so we could see the earlier messages written by Cade. Cameron went to the other messages, almost a dozen.

Cade: Hi, I need some help with science.

User504: Hi Cade, I would love to help you. Can we meet this time, much easier for me?

Cade: Uh, Sure. What works for you?

User504: 34 Baker Street: 5 pm.

Cade: Okay thanks.

Cameron broke in. "I don't think this is him. It's too obvious." He put the phone down and turned around to the shelves.

"What do you mean?"

"She was on her way to my house in the night. They were supposed to meet at 5."

"How do you know she didn't kidnap her later? Cade went missing the 24th, this chat is the 12th." Picking up the phone, going back to the message I looked to the date of the chat.

October 12: 3:30pm

"That makes sense- they could have been talking after." Cameron said putting the phone into his back pocket.

"Don't do that!" Grabbing it back, I blew on it having no idea if it would help or not. "They are going to know someone took it. Here." I grabbed a pen from the desk and a post it, writing the following; user504, October 12, 3:30pm, 34 Baker Street

"Right, smart." he smirked.

A noise then sparked our distraction from Cade and we were right back to this surreal situation. " Hell, not now. I thought you said they weren't going to be here."

"When did I say that?" Cameron hid on the other side of

the desk. I peeked my head up and saw Cameron's mom walking with another police officer. I ducked down and sped over to his side of the desk.

'What are we gonna do?" Turning to Cameron who was in lip distance. I gulped as I saw his soft curved lines, a glimmer on the corner of his lip. Looking down at the floor, I hoped the footsteps in the background would fade away. Cameron was still staring at me. *Don't do it Cameron, please don't.* But, he did. Cameron moved in toward me and my cheat sheet was beginning- he touched back.

For whatever it's worth, She's dead?

Chapter 5

I released and, my foolish heart, finally caught up to my brain. "How are we gonna get out?"

I ignored this mistake.

"Right, um." He looked to the window where he saw no one. "Let's go, don't forget the post- it."

"Yeah, I have it." I followed Cameron to the left side of the police wing. Tip-toeing was much harder than expected; as I told you, I have a habit of stomping. We watched for any other movement in the station while we made our escape. Cameron thought to move without the flashlight. He was right, don't get me wrong. But damn, it was hard to see.

As we neared the parking lot door, my nerves calmed down and my legs ran to the door faster than me. "We did it." Cameron sighed.

"Yeah, I did *it*," referring back to the kiss. I wiped my head and rubbed my shoulders to make them warm. The coldness created condensed puffs of chilled breathes that disappeared within seconds. Watching Cameron turn on the car and heat up the engine was music to my ears. Well, almost music. My mind kept circling on my mistake. Why I would betray Cade? Could she have seen us? Like, from the "beyond?"

Cameron drove out of the parking lot while I reviewed the post-it. Repeating in my mind 34 Baker Street, 34 Baker Street. "We should go check this out." I practically said oblivious to thinking he wouldn't already know that.

"Yeah, Good idea," he said trying to sound like it was the first he had heard it.

I raised back my seat and looked to the right outside the window. The rain started to drizzle in, "God Cade, where are you?"

Chapter 6

"What?" Cameron said while I turned my head to face him.

"Nothing, I'm just tired." I raised up my chair because we were close to home. The rain poured harder now and the sound of it hitting the car settled my body. There was a rhythm that made me calmer and unaware of what I was going to see in front of me, I smiled because Cameron and I had a lead on this case.

A horizontal figure caught my attention. Tall and average weight walking slowly through the pouring rain made my eyes raw. As we zoomed in closer I knew who it was: Cade. "Stop!" I turned the wheel, off to the side trying to go anywhere but in the middle. The pull of the car rocking me back and forth made me nauseous. I let go of the wheel and headed towards the right side of the road bumping into some cars. I turned around and saw Cade, her spirit vanishing, while my heart was cracking.

Synopsis of Car accident: I broke two ribs, while Cameron suffered a mild concussion. We ended up staying in the hospital for a week. When I got better, I started admitting to my parents that I could see Cade. That was a stupid move. They grew concerned with me and sent me to a mental hospital. Cameron went back to school and that was the end of it, until now.

Timeline: One month later

"Nikki!" I popped my head up from the softness of my pillow. I yawned and wiped my eyes. "Nikki!" My name called through the closet door. Getting up, I lost my balance. The hardness of the wooden floor reminded me of my sad reality. The walls of a mental hospital truly separated me from the outside world; and Cade, so I thought.

"Where are you?!" It almost felt like Cade was touching me, shaking my shoulders. She felt so real and for a second I lost myself in possibility of her touch.

"I saw you, I didn't want to hurt you, so I drove to the side. I'm here now."

"Supposed to find me! Told you to find me." She looked at her arms; bruised and red. She still wasn't making complete sentences.

"What is he doing to you?" I asked.

"No consent."

I grew uncomfortable, my body shivered for a few seconds and I imagined him raping her. The thought grossed me out. I tried to wipe it away like erasing something on paper, but it was too haunting to let go of.

"Told me going to help me," her eyes sparkling.

"Help you with what?" I picked up on her missing words.

"Hel-." Cade looked around. "Coming. Need to go. You close. Our string." Her spirit faded away.

Hearing steps coming in, I closed the closet door. I rushed and plopped myself back onto my bed, pulling the sheets over my head. The wooden floor creaked and the noises from outside told me someone was in my room. "Nikki, it is time for your therapy session."

Two words. Bor-ing. I hadn't gotten anywhere with my therapist; she was always asking me about my relationships with Cade, Cameron and Ash. Like "who was closer to you, how do you feel about losing Cade, etc?" Her name was Betty Singer. Betty was in her mid 50s. She was smart, generous and had a soft tone to her voice (made me want to fall asleep). You knew she meant well, but she had no idea what I was dealing with. Nor, believed me. Yes, I did tell her about my confrontations with Cade. How couldn't I? I can't just ignore her questions or respond with one word answers. I started seeing Betty three days after my admission. To make my parents happy, I didn't argue and kept my mouth shut. It's not like I could escape from this place. It was hell. And I was bound.

A few days after talking to her, she showed me a way to express my feelings. Her idea was to write how I felt in a journal every night. She would look at it the next session, which was about every two days. So, the thing is. I was gonna be released two weeks in, but Betty discovered my feelings hidden at the end of my journal. Therefore, another two weeks were added and I still see her soft wrinkled face.

Wait. Before I continue, I need to tell you about the journal. This is what Betty *wanted*.

"I don't really like it here. The walls are not high enough and the comforters barely keep me warm at night."

This is what I *said*.

34 Baker street, 34 Baker street. Cade is there. Missing October 24th. Messages on the 12th. She is still alive. She talked to me. I will find you Cade."

Betty walked in with her black high heels and dotted pant suit. "Hello Nikki."

"Hi." I sat up from the bed; took my oversized hoodie and walked with Betty to the office.

There were two black leather chairs in the middle of the room, a cute rug and decorative paintings. The white noise machine always made my eyes wander off because it lifted all my thoughts from my exploding brain. I sat on the comfortable chair and thought about what Cade said. "You are close." The sentence repeated in my mind. I was on the right track and I needed to tell Cameron. Her voice disrupted my thought.

"Hi, Nikki, how are you feeling?"

"I'm okay."

"Are you still upset with me about the journal?"

I didn't respond. My eyes glued to the floor. My thumbs rolling around each other.

"I'm sorry. It was in your best interest."

I took a deep breathe. I looked up. "Can we get on with the session?"

"Have your parents thought anymore about Meds?"

"No, but either way, I am not gonna do it."

"Alright then, let's carry on."

I wasn't against taking Meds. They could have helped me sleep better, but I was too worried I would lose my connection with Cade.

"Have you seen Cade?" Betty was trying to trick me. I played dumb.

"No, I haven't, I don't really remember saying I did."

"What do you mean you don't remember?"

"Why would I see Cade if she is dead?" I crossed my feet onto the chair.

"So you haven't seen Cade at *all*?" Betty's tone raised, she was questioning suspiciously. I had to convince her.

"Positive, I promise." I crossed my fingers in my lap so she couldn't see.

"We are going to play a game. I am going to say a word, you tell me the first thing that pops into your head."

"Okay."

"Letter."

"C." Darnet, I shouldn't have said that.

"Number."

Here's my chance.

"22." Instead of 34.

"Friend." She said.

"Cameron." I wanted to say Cade.

"Light." The final card.

"Dark." The definition of my whole world.

Chapter 7

This is stupid. My life is stupid. How can Cade still be alive? How am I alive? Why hasn't God taken me yet? Is there something about me Cade doesn't have? Why did he choose? Choosing is wrong. Choosing is hard. Hard isn't the right word. Maybe challenging? No, I'm using hard. Why must hard be life? No, that isn't right. Why must life be hard? Ok, better. But why must everything be hard? Life is a rollercoaster that is for sure, but I just don't get it. How does the future unfold? Will it unfold for me? Badly? Oh, how maybe just ending my life is the best way out.

Our meeting was over within 30 minutes. Suicide was only an idea. Nothing more could be made from it. Maybe a knife. A blade. A pin. But that was stupid thinking of me. I was overexaggerating what people would probably say after hearing about my decision. Nothing could have helped with my choice. Bullshit- so many things could have. But that is only future thinking. I didn't know if Betty saw through my act; I had no idea what she was going to do with me, keep me prisoner for more weeks or let me be a commoner among these hideous people.

Walking back to my room, the nurse told me my mother was on the phone. I was visited around four times by my parents, it may not seem like a lot, but it was all they allowed. We were allowed to hug and everything, but I wasn't so pleased to see them. Not after putting me through this. It was something

I didn't think I would let go of. What hurt the most was that they didn't believe me.

I changed directions and entered a small room. The room shaped like a square had leather black seating where a phone was attached next to the seat. Hearing the other people talk on the phone always annoyed me. I felt self-conscious talking about things while other people were "listening." All the noise and limited space made my temperature rise. I was heated and wiped the formation of dripping sweat off my face. Sitting down, I skidded on the black leather to the farthest I could go. The chairs were about five feet away from each other, but since there were so many people at a time, everyone raised their voice. I covered my mouth over the phone so my mother could hear me. I clawed the ugly, dirty old fashioned phone and started to talk. "Hi." I spoke, hardly feeling anything. It took a lot in me to start a conversation with my mother, again, after sending me to this psychotic place.

"Hi, honey." She said in her gentle tone.

"Hi." I had no purpose to speed up the conversation.

"Nikki, your father and I would really like you to go on meds."

"Mother, I don't think that is a good idea."

Shoot.

"Just because, they might have a side effect." I lied, though it was a possibility.

"The doctor wouldn't put you on something that wasn't safe."

"I don't know, mom."

"Can you at least try them for me?"

She pulled the mother card. Nope, I couldn't let her

have it. I thought of the anger. How I was so mad at her, for everything.

"No, mom. I don't want to have anything."

"Well, your therapist thinks it is a good idea." She paused. "Since you will be staying another two weeks." Mother's voice fainted in the background. The words got smaller and quieter every time I repeated them in my mind. There it was again, the thought of suicide.

"What, how come?" My eyes started to water. The girl near me cocked her head. A look passed her intimidating face, strong and muscular body. I rolled my eyes and looked down at the floor.

"She is worried that, well, you aren't telling the truth."

Dammit.

"I don't know how she could think that. I specifically told her I cannot see her, and never did."

"Are you lying to me?" My mother said.

Mhm. What was I going to say? Lying was an option, so was telling the truth. I usually told the truth except when times called for lying. It seemed like lying was actually all I was doing. So why stop now?

"No, I am not." I kept my voice still; crossed my fingers between my legs (just in case)

"Ok. I just want the best for you. I know it is still shocking. Also the police… they found some possible suspects. I wanted you to hear it from me. I will let you know if anything changes."

How could the police find anything? I guess they had their own strategies, and possibly could have looked through Cade's phone.

"Ok, thanks mom."

"Don't worry, only two more weeks left."

Weeks. The word had a clear denotation. *A boring measure of time that has transformed my life into a living hell.*

"Yeah." I gulped. "Talk to you soon."

I hung up the phone without hearing a response. The walls directed me back to my room; where my single bed with plain white covers was waiting for me. The indentation from the hard bottoms left a square mark. My feet hung over the end of the bed where I lay back and looked to the ceiling. I put my fingers together and tried holding them up to my eye. Bored out of my mind; making shapes and singing to myself. My favorite song was "Immortals" by Fallout Boy. Don't ask me why, but something about the song was magic. His voice could stretch from a low to a high, lighting up the room. The lyrics were about people together facing the world as one, conquering it. I always felt immortal; it hit me pretty hard when I found out I wasn't.

"I try to picture me without you." Singing was a passion of mine. I was pretty good, but cracked a few times here and there. My mother always wanted me to do the school plays, but I told her I wasn't good enough nor did I really want to.

"But I can't." A voice sang.

"Ah." I jumped up from my bed and turned around to see Cade sitting on the chair.

"You always loved that song."

"I still do." I forced a chuckle. Wait. "What, Cade, what are you doing here?"

"The suspects, they aren't right. There is a henchmen but it isn't the guy." It was easier to understand Cade now.

"Are you okay?"

"I'm fine for now, just please- go get help."

"How? I am locked up here."

"Well Nick, for starters you can tell the police."

If I told the police, questions would arise again. Like "how would I know? "where did you hear this from?" or "have you seen this person before?" Also, Cade knew why I was here. Therefore, telling the police wasn't an option to me.

"Nikki, I know what you are thinking, why would they believe you after telling about me? But- I still think you should."

I crossed my feet.

"Ok, I will think about it. But bad news Cade."

She sat on the couch twiddling her thumbs then looked up when my voice rested on the bad. Cade's expression told me to continue.

"I have to stay here for another two weeks."

Cade smiled; then laughed. "Yeah, I know that. That's why Cameron is going to bust you out of here."

How would Cade know? I knew she couldn't read minds. Hold up, Cameron getting me out of a mental hospital? There were fences around this place. Security guards at every corner, every hour. There was one outside my room who checked on me every night. "Everything ok Nikki?" his deep toned voice would say. How was a teenage boy supposed to get into a insane asylum without getting caught?

I know what you're thinking- with me." Cade smiled and her spirit vanished.

A knock on the door. I awoke from my peaceful sleep. "Yes?"

The nurse came in with some magazines and letters. My

parents wrote letters occasionally. It's not like they had anything new to say to me. I knew my routine and my time here. If anything were to change they would either call, or someone else would tell me. Today, officially, marks a week and three days until I'm out of here. But what was Cade telling me? I hadn't seen her since four days ago so that couldn't be a good sign. Remembering her bruises and the misconfiguration of her body; I shivered. Cade was a strong person, but I knew anything like this would tear her apart, I'm sure it would for anyone.

"Here you go Ms. Field. A letter." The nurse dropped the envelope on my bed. I hesitated to grab it. The ink was blue and my name was scripted on the cover with a heart on the top of my name. My hands ripped the sides open and I pulled the letter out. White and small decorations surrounded the entire envelope. My eyes looked to the top and in bubble letters spelled: Nick. I instantly knew who wrote it, Ash. What would he have to say though? Clearly, he didn't believe me and I knew he probably didn't care what my life was like now. Anyway, I began reading.

Nikki,

Its Ash. I am sorry I haven't talked to you in a while. I really didn't know if it was a good idea to reach out to you, but I wanted to. I heard about the crash and I hope you are okay. I never meant to hurt you. I hope the treatment is working and that you are hanging in there. I really do miss you. Maybe I will see you soon, Nick.

Ash.

There it was again. Nick. He called me that once before on the phone after finding out what I've been doing with Cade.

A tinge of a smile grew upon my face that I couldn't resist. He still cared about me. Then a wash of sadness devoured it. Ash *still* didn't believe me. I tried to balance my feelings so I wouldn't cry. Truly, I did miss him and even though he didn't believe me, I missed the way I felt with him. But "I hope the treatment is working" was like a dagger in my mind. Somehow I wanted to stick it farther so it wouldn't hurt anymore, but then I'd die.

It was around 10 in the morning and my noise machine was whirring causing me to feel drowsy. I always had trouble sleeping. My mind would always wonder and think about something; other times it would just blank. There was no way to help me, I even tried counting sheep and that made it even worse. One of my friends told me to take Melatonin and I have ever since. Thankfully, this medication didn't stop me from seeing Cade.

The nurse came back with a tray full of food. I usually had to get up and walk to the cafeteria to eat. "From Ash." The nurse smiled and placed the heavenly food on my lap. This time it was filled with croissants and cereals. Not that other crappy food they served that made me want to puke. Ash knew I loved all this stuff. I was obsessed with banana bread and when I found it on the tray, I kind of squealed. The nurse laughed and I looked up already stuffing the food into my ravenous mouth. There was milk on the side filled to the top of a glass. I drank it down and gulped a sigh of relief once the banana bread settled in my stomach. "I'm glad you like it." The nurse said folding the blanket at the end of my bed. I ate a few other pieces before the nurse took the tray away. Silently, I wished Ash a thank you. The nurse wiped my face with a towel, but before finishing I told her I could do it. Everyone took it a little too extreme at this place. I was here for "mental purposes" not a disorder where I couldn't take care of myself. Yet, the extra attention was nice at times.

"What do I have going on today?" I stopped the nurse before she could make it out the door. She turned around and checked her schedule that was stowed in her right side pocket.

"Well, you do not have your therapist today so you can read, take a walk, and tonight the whole community is going to watch a movie." If someone told me that they were stuck watching a movie with other people they didn't know I would feel sorry for them. Except now that I'm in this situation and haven't been under the influence of having a tv in arms reach whenever I wanted, my heart kind of jumped. I hoped they would pick something that was funny. I loved comedies, especially horror films. But- right now horror films would not be the best thing to watch. When I was with Cade, I used to force her to watch scary movies. She used to grab my arm whenever something popped out, but we would always laugh it off. Whenever we finished, Cade would thank me that I forced her to. Though, comedies were really our all time favorite genre. We would always come up with inside jokes and make each other laugh randomly at school. My favorite was 21 Jump Street; I would think to say Cade's was Bridesmaids or Pitch Perfect.

"Okay, thanks." I reviewed the letter once more and set it aside on the counter.

I put my clothes on and tightened my pony tail. My brown hair ran a little dry because of the dead ends. Nobody had cut my hair in over two months and the unevenness was getting annoying. One side would always be a little longer than the other, and not that it was noticeable, it was just something I wanted to get rid of. The nurse came in and smiled "Ready to go?"

I looked into the mirror one last time, "Yup." That was the first time I was excited about something. I hadn't been out of this place in a few days, so it was nice to get some fresh air. My heart was beating fast and I was ready to explore the outside.

"Here she is." My heartbeat stopped. I looked over to the side of me and the security guard stood in his tight form.

"What?" I babbled out.

"Dmitry is coming on the walk with you."

I shrugged. I thought it was finally going to be me against the world. Well not physically, but you know what I mean. Finding out I needed someone to stalk me the whole time wasn't great news. In fact, I almost started walking by myself to see if I could make it out the door before he followed. Though, It wasn't the best idea.

"Oh okay." I faked a smile, then looked back at the nurse. "How long can I be out for?"

She checked her watch and looked at Dmitry. "It's 12 now, you can get some lunch with her and be back after." The nurse walked over and handed him some cash. When she said I could get lunch, I bit my lip, thinking of a good thick crusted well done slice of pizza that I was going to devour.

"Thank you." I thought it would be okay to start walking. The cold breeze filled my lungs. Then the urge of wanting to ride a motorcycle hijacked my thoughts. The image of Ash and me riding in the wind paused my movement. I stood still and closed my eyes trying to pinpoint any noise of an engine.

Anything that would cause me to feel the least bit sane. Then there it was. A black one with a strip of red metallic passed in front of me. I opened my eyes and for a second thought it was Ash. I jolted forward and could see Dmitry follow behind me reaching out his arm. The motorcycle stopped in front and he pulled off his helmet; he smiled and walked away. My heart sank, 1 percent of me hoped it could have been him. Maybe he was going to visit me, but that was a stupid thought.

I continued walking straight and looped around a couple times. Dmitry hadn't been over me like my shadow on a sunny day. Sometimes I forgot he was there and walked too fast; he would say my name and I would stop and apologize.

I grabbed a small towel as soon as we got back. The towel wiped all the sweat from my face while I chugged a bottle of water down my throat. Dmitry had gone to change and shower; the nurse told me I needed to also. I quickly changed into my robe and put my hair down. My hands brushed through to try to detangle it. "Your shower is ready, Ms. Field."

I followed the nurse to the shower area. The bathroom was like a locker room. It had different sections divided for stalls, lockers, and showers. I found my locker and put my robe, sandals and ponytail in the corner; put the code in and shut it. The nurse started the shower for me. The hospital provided essentials like conditioner and shampoo for the patients. To be honest, they were good products. My hair was a little frizzy but it's been good. "You have 15 minutes, I will be outside if you need anything."

Thank god. She was going to leave me alone. I waited for the door to shut before I started singing. "I've been staring at the edge of the water, long as I can remember, never really knowing why." The words left my mouth with a beautiful melody. Moana was one of my favorite movies. The sea was one of my favorite things ever. I always imagined myself sailing through the ocean with my family. It was a place where I could feel peaceful and alone. Sometimes being alone isn't a bad thing. You can learn things from yourself. Whenever my mom or dad told me to be with family I simply said "maybe later." I loved being by my window seat staring at the sky. I used to write in my diary but it seemed pointless because no one would ever read it. I know a diary is supposed to be for yourself, but there was always something inside of me that wanted people to read how I felt. I had a voice and something to tell the world; I wanted people to hear it.

I took the vanilla scented soap and scrubbed it on my legs and body. Usually, to let the frizz go down, I would keep the conditioner in my hair for a few minutes. The nurse came in, " five more minutes left, then we are going to go down and watch the movie."

I rinsed the conditioner out of my hair, " I wish, I could be the perfect daughter but I come back to the water, no matter how hard I try." My voice cracked at the end. "Ugh." I always cracked and it annoyed the crap out of me.

I stopped the shower and wrapped the towel around me. Entering the code to my locker, I grabbed all my belongings and opened the door on the way out. "All done?" The nurse smiled.

I was getting sick of the smiling, but I knew she was only trying to be friendly. I nodded and we continued walking to my room. Before leaving, the nurse closed the curtains and put my clean clothes on the bed. "The movie is starting soon."

I combed my hair with my old brush; I was allowed to take a few things from home with me, if they weren't "dangerous." You can't possibly tell me that a hair brush would be categorized as that, so I took it. The nurses hadn't even noticed I snuck it in with a couple of other things.

"What movie?" I lay the brush down on my bedside table.

"The Parent Trap, do you like that movie?"

I nodded and grabbed my clothes from my bed. The door shut behind me as I waited until no one was longer in the room. My shorts and shirt were soft and warm like they just been pressed. I quickly changed outfits and braided my hair to the left side. The nurse had been waiting outside; she handed me a water for the movie. We walked over together to the lower level of the center. There was a big area where a screen came down and seating area was arranged with foam blocks and bean bags. If there were elderly people, there were cushioned seats sitting against the end of the wall. It was a pretty nice size space.

I was able to choose my own bean bag and place it anywhere across the room. Sitting in any corner was my favorite. In school, those were where I focused best. I picked up the big green one and slid it over closer to the right wall. "Need anything, Ms. Field?"

I plopped down, " I'm okay, thank you." My body twisted back and forth trying to find the most comfortable position. My back drew sharp pains and I slid off a little bit hoping it would be more comfortable, it wasn't. The lights became dimmed and one of the nurses announced the movie and its running time. Two hours for me to be relaxed and let my brain roam free. I hadn't been happy here. Especially if people found out where I had been these past weeks. My parents and the school had came up with a plan to tell everyone. They discussed the car crash and how my injuries were more serious than Cameron's. It would be my worst nightmare if anyone found out I was here, well except for Cameron, and now Ash, I guess.

The movie was about an hour in. The two girls discovered they were sisters and swapped places. No matter how many times I've seen it, this movie would never get old. Cade and I have seen this movie so many times; every sleepover we would watch it. Well, not every sleepover, but it was a lot. As I was watching the movie I heard a knock on the window behind me. I looked to see Cameron standing up motioning me to come outside. I was in shock at the unexpected visit. Could it be another ghost or head mistake? How was I supposed to even get out there? Wait. I got it. I took a sip of my water and quietly exited the room. Trying to find my nurse took a while, there were so many within the place. Finally, I found her having a cup of tea at the cafeteria. "Hi." I cupped my hands behind my back. The nurse looked up and smiled.

"Everything okay?" She lay down her glass.

"Yes, I was wondering if I could go on a walk." I looked down at the ground to add an emotional effect. "I-I need some air."

The nurse got up and rubbed my back. "Sure, let me go get Dmitry." The nurse motioned me to follow her. My plan was working, but I needed to convince Dmitry to let me go off on my own. As I caught up with the nurse, I thought about what to say. I've been told the best way to get out of a situation is to tell the truth. Though, I wasn't sure in this case that idea was the best. Dmitry showed up with his sunglasses and black sweatpants and tank top.

"Sorry, Dmitry."

"It's okay, Nick." He smiled.

It was weird hearing my nickname from an adult. I was used to people my age calling me it, but I connected with Dmitry. We had talked and been through everything together. Well, he helped me a lot let's just say. We continued walking out the door, I scouted for any sign of Cameron. As we made it far enough away from the hospital, I stopped. "Dmitry, would you mind if I went on my own?" I didn't know if that was good enough. He didn't change his dull expression. I hoped telling the truth would make me more trustworthy so I went with my gut. " Dmitry, please let me go talk to my friend." His blank expression slowly changed into an evil smile, like the Grinch. It looked like he knew what I wanted to do.

"Go talk a walk on your own, five minutes." He gave me a little push and whistled away. I sprinted as fast I could softly calling Cameron's name. He wasn't behind the first bush, and walking to the second I ducked when I was in front of the window. "Cameron!" I demanded to know where he was. I heard a rustle behind one and out came Cameron who tugged me into his arms. I was in shock he came to see me, but I hugged back. My grip was holding onto him so tight; I let go and looked up at him. " How did you get past the gate?"

"You remember the guy Thomas, he was in our math class?"

"The really smart dude?"

Cameron laughed and walked around me. " Yeah, that one. So I got a device that you put on your back. It makes you invisible on any sort of detecting system." Then he took out an object from his pocket; it was rectangle and shiny. "Thomas made a copy of a card so I could get into the building if anyone asked me who I was."

I looked at Cameron's picture. It was pretty recent and under his name it said he worked as a janitor for the hospital.

"I can't believe you." I pushed him.

"Yeah, you are also not going to believe what else I did." Confusion passed my face and I looked to the rustling bush. The sneakers were first to catch my attention; bright blue with black surrounding the outside. My eyes made its way up and they were almost knocked out by my amount of surprise. Ash was standing with his hands in his pockets looking at Cameron, like he didn't know what to say.

"What is going on guys?" I said totally objecting the idea of reaching in for a hug. Cameron came closer to me. I didn't have much time left for him to speak. His face looked serious as he checked the time on this watch.

"We are going to get you out." Ash broke in. Cameron stopped his focus and stuck the middle finger out at Ash, I laughed. Wait. Back up a sec.

"What the hell you mean you are going to get me out?" I tapped my foot up and down hoping Dmitry wasn't eavesdropping.

"Cade left me a sign- she." I could see her name was hitting him hard. " She managed to leave a note."

I turned to Ash to see if he was buying this. "What do you mean Cade? You never mentioned anything about her?" His words spoke of disbelief. My stomach churned.

"What did it say?" My eyes lighting up.

"Get Nikki out now- I will know when and will help you."

Cade had done it. She was right, like she said, she did it. But how was she supposed to get me out? What did I will help you mean?

Out of nowhere Cade's spirit appeared. "Ah." I looked to the left of me.

"What?!" Ash's face looked worried.

"Let me guess, Cade?" Cameron smiled.

"Damn, he's getting good at this." Cade laughed, so did I. I didn't say that to Cameron because he hadn't asked.

"Cade I don't know how much time I have left, Dmitry is going to come back."

"Tell Cameron to tell you the plan." I repeated her demand and as wished he followed.

"We are going to come back in two days, Ash and I. Come out to the door or as far as you can. Cade said she will do the rest. Oh, that was also on the card."

"Ouch!" Cade twinged and looked at her arm. A bright bruise suddenly appeared. Her eyes in horror. " I have to go, this will help you, tell Ash that I said he loves you and has for a long time."

With that, her spirit vanished and I heard the murmur of a cry. My eyes started to water. Cameron came over and hugged me.

"What happened, Nick?"

"I think-she's getting whipped." O-M-G. Those words. Whipped. I could only imagine how much it must have hurt. Why was this guy doing this to her? What did he want? My endless stream of sadness became dark and angry. I let go of Cameron.

"You know what? I am sick that you don't believe me. Your pity letter was nothing". My voice was angry, most it's ever been at Ash. He started to walk away. "Don't believe me. But Cade told me to tell you that she said you loved me- and have for a while." I wiped the tears from my eyes, but noticed Ash stopped and walked back. Cameron nudged me on the arm, this was a sign that what I said was true, and helpful.

"What did you just say?"

"You heard me- you are in love with me."

"But- how would."

I cut him off, " I told you, Cade told me." The whole world just turned upside down for him. His eyes looked like they figured out the missing piece of the puzzle. I couldn't tell if he was happy or mad that I had known his feelings towards me. To be honest, I hadn't thought about it being a possibility.

"What do you have to say for yourself, Ash." Cameron said with an eager tone.

My five minutes was way up, but Dmitry was nowhere in sight. " I'm- I'm sorry Nikki." He looked down at the ground. Like he had done the worst thing possible. I started to cry, happy and sad tears. Sad he never believed me, but happy that Cade had enough time to tell me. " I should have believed you. God I'm such a bad boyfriend." I couldn't look at his moving mouth any longer, I ran as fast as I could and jumped on him. Our kiss was long and full. I hadn't kissed anyone in over a month and it felt amazing.

Cameron made a noise after it had been a few seconds. I jumped off him and hugged Ash for a tight second. " We are coming back in two days. Be ready."

He started walking away with Ash following. " Bye Nick, I

love you." That was the phrase when everything was supposed to feel great. There were two ways to respond, either say it back or awkwardly thank the guy. I had no time to reply when I turned to see a glimpse of Cameron's face decrease in happiness. That look reminded me of the time I ignored Cameron's kiss, then that image reminded me that I still needed to tell Ash. Ugh, whenever something seemed to get better it always ended with a stake in the heart. And this one was going to hurt everyone.

Chapter 8

The boys rushed past the window running to the other side, while I heard Dmitry's footsteps getting closer to me. I turned around, " Thank you." He nodded and we went back inside to the movie room. The movie was close to the end; the families were coming together to be one again. The twins had once again saved their parents relationship. I knew almost every word and still found a way to never get bored.

I didn't know what to expect; whether or not they were going to able to get me out. It sounded crazy that Cade was going to help. What time was everything supposed to happen? I mean, the nighttime was probably the best, but still they never mentioned specifics. Tomorrow was the day I was going to leave this place. Break free from all this crap about stopping my communication with Cade. Because knowing one thing about me was: I was as stubborn as a mule.

I packed a few of my belongings in a bag by my bed. Nothing too noticeable, but about two shirts and my brush. I hoped Cameron or Ash would think to bring more things for me. This escape was eating me up, I couldn't tell anyone, which was fine, but I was going to miss Dmitry. Especially because they would question him after my absence. The only thing I could think of that would make me feel better was a letter. Short and sweet was what my mom always told me when writing letters, and it worked for most of the time. I found a pen and notepad next to my bed; it was always there and sometimes before bed I would write to myself.

Dmitry,

Please do not say anything. I am so sorry to put you in this position, but I can't stay here. Whether you believe me about Cade, I can't convince you anymore than I've tried. I will miss you sooo much. You were a friend and great body guard.

Nick.

I curled up the note and then slipped it into the drawer. My heart began to beat fast, as I was nervous about this whole plan. "Hello?" The nurse spoke outside the door. Before answering she charged in and smiled with a glass of milk. " Here, fresh and warm."

"Thank you, Daisy." I quickly grabbed the cup and gulped it down. It had been so long since I've had milk, well especially warm milk. But why were they being so nice to me?

"Why are you doing this?" I asked.

She chuckled. " Whenever it's the last week we treat the patient with some goods."

This made me feel guilty. I was going to ditch my program and leave everyone who cared for me behind. For a second, I wasn't sure this was a good idea, but then again, all these people thought I was crazy so what the hell did I have to lose anyway? "Thank you, Daisy. For everything."

She smiled. "Of course, honey. I'm glad you are feeling better." My stomach twisted. The feeling of stupidity and insanity filled my body, "Feeling better?" Another person making me sound like I had gone off the edge. That phrase made me sound like an ill person who was treated for a disease. I know I was in this hell hospital, but I was *not* insane.

"And, you have your therapist tonight for the last time."

I totally forgot about her; I sighed my way back into the covers and lay the glass down on the side of my bed.

"I will give you some time to rest before she comes." The nurse exited the room and I was left in a silence. The whispers on the walls constantly interrupted my peaceful thoughts. I was anxious to leave, it was insane to think a missing girl and two teenagers could get me out of here. Why was my life like this? Why did God hurt my best friend and take away my love for everyone? I missed Cade; everything about my life was different now, if you couldn't tell. My own mother and father betrayed me. My boyfriend finally came to his senses but it made me question whether to trust him again in the future. A relationship was supposed to be built on honesty and trust; what if something like this happened again? What if I needed to tell Ash about something and he didn't believe me once again? All these things were meant to be talked out by a therapist, but I couldn't trust Betty. She would terminate my rights to leave soon, not that that mattered anyway.

"Ms. Field." The knock on the door woke me up.

"Yes?" I yawned and wiped my teary eyes.

The nurse came in with my therapist who was dressed in another playsuit. This one was red and loose in the pants and sides. The v-neck dropped a little lower than usual and her hair slightly touched her shoulders. "Hi, Nikki." She motioned me for us to go into her office.

We came into the room and I plunged my weight onto the black chair. "How is your final week going?" Betty smiled taking out her notebook.

"It's been good, thank you." I tried to act kind and sane.

"What are you most looking forward to?"

"I'm excited to see my mom and dad." I said keeping my friends out of this mess. Her questions could been intrusive and my reaction could have destroyed my escape.

"How are you sleeping?"

I didn't want to sound like there was nothing wrong with me, so I tried to make conversation. "It is hard to fall asleep in the beginning, but once I do I'm fine."

"Is there anything on your mind at all?"

I tightened my posture and pulled the sleeves of my sweatshirt over my thumbs. "I miss Cade sometimes."

"It is normal to, she was your best friend. But I think it is safe to say that you are grieving and handling this tragedy very well."

"Thank you, I agree."

"How is the stress, have you talked to your family?"

"It has been okay, not much communication between my family since the time I've been here."

She wrote down some notes and ripped the page off. "When you get home, here is a list of things I think you should try. Might help with your feelings and appetite. The nurse's have told me you are eating better so I don't want that to change."

I took the note and folded it into my sweatshirt.

Thankfully, that was the last session I would ever have to go through. I took the slip of paper from my sweatshirt and threw it in the garbage bin. I didn't need help on what to eat, heck I didn't need help with anything. I just needed a few people to believe my story, and I now I had that.

The light outside was darkening within the hour. It was

around 7 pm and my eyes were starting to close. It was early, but being bored most of the time made me tired. My stomach rumbled a couple of times and I snuck a fruit or two earlier on. I had a few bites of an apple and covered it in a towel so they wouldn't see. I'm sure they wouldn't be mad that I took it, but maybe they think I was binging on food and that I had another problem yet to be sorted out.

Getting into bed I could feel the warmth of the sheets hit my body. The softness of the pillow against my neck put me in a comfortable position; I ignored all my arousing thoughts and focused on my sleep. I kept changing my position every time another thought stopped me from achieving idleness. The bed grew more and more uncomfortable and I eventually slept on the opposite side of the bed. The heat was getting into my body and one thing I hate is sleeping in the heat. I always slept in the cold no matter where. At Cade's house I would always turn her fan on because I couldn't stand being buried under her covers without a breeze blowing in my face. She thought I was insane, but in a good way.

As my body rested over the sheets and the air cooled my body down I was soon drifting into a blank space.

"Nikki, get up!" A voice erupted my sleep and I shot up from the covers.

"Huh?" I wiped the crust from my eyes.

"They are here, get up!"

Dammit. I slept too late. I grabbed the bag with my clothes and tossed the pillow on the other side of the bed. Quietly running to the door, Cade directed me to the spot. "Where are we going?" I asked running by her side.

"Just follow me." She took my hand and pulled me after

her. We walked past the dark hallways filled with emptiness. Every corner I thought a nurse would come out with a flashlight and blind my eyes. I could replay the scene in my head of me screaming my way off of the police and Dmitry looking at me in the eyes. Wait. Shoot, the letter. I stopped quickly and ran to the other side of the hallway to his room. He lived alone so I didn't need to worry about any other people finding the letter before he did. "What are you doing, Nikki?" Cade demanded.

"Just wait," I spoke a little sass, but Cade knew I didn't mean it as an insult.

Her shaky voice and heavy breath reminding me that we were in a hurry. My heart was beating ten times faster than usual and I thought there was a possibility I could pass out.

We cut corners and kept our voices quiet. I finally saw Cameron and Ash from the distance with strong, but worried faces. Cameron waved his hand and I smiled that they had gotten past everything. "Wait, how did they not see you if you're in the hospital?"

"I told you I would help you- I broke the electricity."

I had no idea Cade was capable of that. "How did you even do that?"

"No time to explain." Her tone grew strict.

Cameron grabbed my hand and Ash took the bag from my shoulder. "Let's go. I have stuff in the car for you. "

"Where are we going?" I had no idea what else was involved. Where would we go? How long would we be there for?

"Just don't talk and listen." Ash said. Damn, I gotta say that kind of made me happy. His voice sometimes gave me the chills when it was a really tense moment. This was that moment. I smiled and continued walking with the both of them.

We made a couple turns and landed in front of the door and desk. "Put this on." Cameron said taking something out of his backpack. It looked like a ball with straps around the sides. I put my hands through the holes and in the center stood the ball a little below my chest. I didn't ask any questions because there was no time. Ash came over to me and pressed the blue button on the top of the ball. "Ok, let's go. We are going straight to the car."

We blasted straight out of the hospital, running. It was cold and my body was freezing. I looked for Cade around but she was nowhere in sight. "Where the hell is Cade?" I yelled calling for her.

"How would I know? I can't see her." Cameron said.

That was a little harsh, but I ignored the comment. I got in the car and closed the door. Ash threw my bag in the back and I saw the other ones along the seat. I reached in to look for a blanket; when I found one, my body tingled. The blanket was soft and pink. It was from my bed at home and Cameron knew it was my favorite.

"Are you okay?" Ash said when him and Cameron were in the car.

I sniffed. "Yeah I'm fine, let's just get out of here." Cameron started the car and when we started moving, I was never happier to leave a place before. I hoped Dmitry would get my note and his career would be okay. I lay across the back seat and stared out the window. The night sky always astounded me. I wish I could fly because I always loved the wind in my face and the cold. As my body trembled trying to get warm, I wasn't up to asking what would happen next. I lost my eyes to the idea of sleep and off they went without me.

"Nikki, Nick." The sound faded in closer and closer until my eardrums rang.

"What?" I grumbled back at whoever said that. I was still in the car after some time. I guess I needed the sleep because Cameron told me I had been out for an hour.

"Where are we?" I asked taking off the blanket.

"I found a place where we could stay for a while, until we.. if we... uh."

Cameron interrupted him. " We need to stay here if we want to find Cade on our own." he said it perfectly and I could tell Ash was mad and embarrassed at the same time.

"So how long do you think we will be here?"

Cameron scratched his head. "Don't know, I mean clearly Cade is still alive, and needs our help."

"Ok, thanks you guys." I went in to hug Ash and say thank for all that he has done. He once again apologized for being an idiot and rubbed my back. I kissed him on the lips softly and moved on to Cameron. Hugging Cameron so tight, I tried not to force anything that would look suspicious. But without thinking, I gave him a kiss on the check. He smiled and nudged me to start walking. I didn't take the time to look at Ash's face because the remaining memory of kissing Cameron stunned the back of my brain. We walked to the abandoned house with dead trees surrounding the place. The grass was stained with a dark brown rust and the walkway was torn apart. Getting closer, I could smell the scent of oldness and mold. I looked at Ash who kept his face held high and continued walking into the rundown entrance.

"We will sleep in the same room, so we stick together." Cameron said struggling with the bags he held.

I reached over to take a bag from him as we walked up the stairs. The vintage wooden steps creaked almost every step of the way. Following Cameron and Ash, I focused on the torment my parents might be feeling. To know that I could have escaped a hospital and be anywhere was even shocking to myself. We ended up in a large sized room. The house was basic and normal size. There was minimal running water and electricity. This was going to be tough for all of us.

Three beds were split among the room; soft white sheets covered them.

"What do we do now?" Ash said laying my bag on the first bed.

"We find Cade. First we should go to 34 Baker Street and contact the user." I said.

Cameron laughed. "Woah there Nick, you need to rest. We can tomorrow."

"But-"

"No buts." Cameron took off his sweatshirt and picked up the bag. "I am going downstairs to make some food- want a pb and j?"

"Yes please." I jumped into bed and stared at the ceiling.

"I will take one too." Ash said sitting on the edge of my bed.

"What if they find us?" I sat up with my arms behind my back.

"Then we'll run." Cameron smiled walking out of the room.

"Is he joking?" I dropped back down on the bed.

"Duh." Ash punched my foot.

"I will let you rest. I'm gonna go help Cameron." He got off the bed and shut the door behind him. I closed my eyes and took a deep breathe, because I needed one. How did I get here? Why was I seeing Cade? Why was someone after her? Too many questions in such little time; I had enough. My body was aching and I needed to rest more. An hour of sleep was not enough. My body flipped on its stomach and from there I went to sleep.

"Cade!" "Cade!" I was running to her. I could see her getting whipped and beaten by this man. My heart shattered every time the leather belt hit her skin. I tried helping her but a barrier stopped me. It was a powerful force that shut me out everytime my hand touched it. It was invisible so I didn't know it was there at first. Her eyes looking at me was enough to know how she felt. All of the sudden a shift in the string occurred. It wasn't broken, but It ripped me open. I felt her grave becoming marked and the string was about to snap.

I awoke from this nightmare. I hadn't screamed, but my body was racing with heat and sweat. I sighed because my surroundings were the same; I was still in this dusty old room. But I noticed the string was undone. I looked outside from my room where I could hear a banging sound. No one was there but the banging and whipping become louder. I screamed as it was flooding my eardrums. The string was not fully tied like it was previously. "Cade!" "Cade!" I yelled at the top of my lungs because I knew she was in trouble. Without knowing, tears starting rolling down my face and my vision was becoming blurry "No! Cade where the hell are you?!"

Finally I saw Cade at the end of the upstairs hallway. Her

spirit faintly showing, I could almost see through her. She was covered in blood and bruises; rolled up tightly in the corner. Her head tilted to me. "Close your eyes." She managed to say.

My eyes shut to blackness and I saw Cade being whipped by the man.

I realized that wasn't a nightmare, but I was *with* Cade.

I no longer felt insane. I felt psychotic.

Chapter 9

"Stop! Stop hitting her!" I ran over to Cade, following the direction when my eyes were closed. I opened my eyes as I was closer to Cade, but when I came back to reality, she was gone. No banging or whipping; just my brain processing all I thought I believed in, which was Cade was alive.

My knees dropped on the wood floor and the hardness sent a sharp pain up my legs. Cameron and Ash's voice in the background was slowly vibrating my ears. What I witnessed would change the way I felt about the world. Every time I was walking on the street would I feel watched? Afraid to smile at a man, fearing he would take me? I felt a touch on my shoulder and Ash's face looked more worried than ever. He kneeled down to my level and tried to pick me up. I was too heavy; with my state of mind I couldn't get up. Cameron ran to the other side and tried helping. My legs were wiggling and I was falling down again.

The boys pulled me up harder and finally got me up on my two feet. My hands wrapped around their shoulders, walking to the bed. When I made it back up onto the soft pillows, my head spun. The room had titled and my blood pressure was dropping. My eyes were spinning around losing sight of Cameron and Ash; I tried moving my hands to find them both on each side of me.

Next, I felt a needle being injected into my arm. The sharp tip had been enough to make the thought of vomiting an option. I didn't know why Cameron did that, but it seemed to work as I was falling asleep. My last thought before getting lost in the death medicine, was seeing Cade in the corner, broken, like *I* had shattered her glass heart instead of the man.

"Cade." I shot up from the bed. No expression on my face, as I was in shock whether or not I had been dreaming. Cameron and Ash were on their beds listening to music and reading. I closed my eyes over and over again, but I got no where. Just black color. Black light. Black hope.

The light in the room showed me I slept through the night with the help of the sedative. My eyes couldn't hold it in any longer and my mouth opened with what seemed to be a cry. The tears started pouring over me and I got up calling Cade's name. "Nick, Stop." Ash said taking me by the arms. I closed my eyes over and over again.

"Cade." I whispered to myself. Cameron got up and ran over to me; my face still surrounded by water. I dug my body into Cameron and made Ash let go of my arms. Whether or not he was hurt by it, I had no time to think. Cameron had believed me in the end, and I needed my best friend more than ever. He rubbed my back softly.

"It's okay Nick, you are safe." Cameron said.

I cursed. "But Cade isn't!" I screamed even harder, even louder, even madder now. My body felt weak and unbalanced as I was in the arms of Cameron. "I saw Cade, she was getting whipped."

Cameron looked up at Ash. "What- How could you?"

"I- I don't know." My voice strained. It was hard to even imagine how. First I was seeing Cade, then seeing visions, now I could see where she was? What the hell was my mind doing to me? I'm pretty sure it wanted to kill me.

"It was terrible. " I looked at Cameron in the face and let go. "She has bruises all over her." Looking at my hands, like it had been me.

"We need to find her." Ash reassured me.

I don't know why I said this, but I needed food. "Can I please have a sandwich, though?"

Right now didn't feel like the time to laugh, but I guess they were cheering me up. The only thing calling my name besides Cade right now, was a toasted peanut butter and jelly sandwich.

"Yeah, come down."

I picked myself up from the floor and walked alongside the two boys. The sensation of jelly and peanut butter tickling my tongue made my mouth water a little. The kitchen was small and wooden cabinets surrounded the area. An island covered in old marble was built in at the middle of the kitchen. Around four chairs were seated across the side of the island; I picked the one closest to Cameron where he was finishing making my toast.

Stupidly, Cameron picked up the toast and burned himself; it flew a few inches across the table. My hand went after it, I stood up and grabbed the peanut butter and jelly from inside the bags. I hadn't had this in such a long time, and my mom used to make the best ones. My knife dug into the jar and grabbed an amount that was too much for normal people. But everyone knows at this point, I'm not normal.

The crust crunched into my fingers and the jelly and peanut butter melted onto the sides. A little bit was dripping on the edge; I took my finger, slid the jam and snuck it into my mouth. I started eating the sides and then going into the whole thing. Cameron and Ash gave me weird looks while I was devouring it.

"So what are we going to do next?" Ash asked.

Cameron finished his last bite and took the plate to the dishwasher. "I think we need to go to 34 Baker Street."

"Do we even know where that is?" I said.

Ash took out his phone waving it around him. "The signal sucks in here."

Cameron response was equally obnoxious. "You can leave."

My mind laughed. I was drawn to Cameron and his personality. Both he and Ash were alike in so many ways, yet my heart ached to be with Cameron. Nobody knew how bad. I didn't know either until the kiss. We were always friends, it was me, Cade and Cameron. Then Ash came along and we become a foursome. I never knew my feelings would grow for Cameron like this. He had that charm to him, where he could be so annoying and act like a jerk. So could Ash. Now that they were both here, it made it that much harder to be with both of them. My feelings were split equally; I was drawn to them at different times in different places for different reasons.

"Ok, I got it. 34 Baker Street is an hour and 45 minutes away."

"So, when do we go?"

"We leave in 15, gather your clothes and bags."

I walked up to the sink and met Ash who playfully blocked me from putting my plate away. He took me by the arms and wrapped them around me. I remember my uncle doing this to me, and never understood where Ash got it from. I laughed and tried hurting him to let me go.

"Ash, Stop. Let me go." I said seriously without trying to laugh. Cameron was putting the peanut butter and jelly back into the bags and we exchanged looks. My heart bounced and I felt uncomfortable.

I turned around to face Ash. "I've missed this hair." I laughed and let my fingers comb through his golden locks.

His eyes lowered, and his dimples left his beautiful face. "Nick, I am sorry. I should have trusted you."

My hands lifted up his head and we stared into each other's eyes. "Hey, Stop, I forgive you. You're here now." I said. He smiled and leaned in for a kiss. My lips touched back and I realized just how much I missed him. I couldn't control my feelings, and what I said next, was unexpected. I let go of his soft touch. "I love you."

I could see his mouth opening to respond, but we were interrupted by Cameron barging in. "Nikki, check Ash's phone!" Our eyes peered onto his screen.

The words stunned my eyes.

Amber Alert: A female, Nikki Field, has gone missing from State Mental Hospital.

Description: Age 16, Caucasian, dark brown hair, green eyes

Height- 5'6

Weight- 130

It was weird to see a message sent out for me. I had never done something this crazy in my entire life. But this should not be for me. Cade is the one who is truly missing and has been this whole time. She isn't dead, and people don't get that. They should be out there for her. My mind re-imagined the Amber alert.

Amber Alert: A female, Cade Murphy, has gone missing

Description: Age 16, Caucasian, golden brown hair, blue eyes

Height- 5'5

Weight- 135

The thought of my parents, and everyone else thinking this could be the same situation as Cade, sank my heart even lower than it already was. The purpose of leaving the hospital was not to let people think I had run away. I mean, I did run away, but they didn't know what I could do. My ability to communicate with Cade would be the only way I could help her, save her, if that was even a possibility. And it better be one, because I'd be distraught if this was all for nothing.

"Nick, don't worry about it. After we go to 34 Baker street will go to my mother, see what we can do?"

"Wait, you're mom?" I looked at him like he was crazy. His mother was a police officer, and going to her and actually being a runaway, just made it even worse an idea.

"Yes, trust me. Let's just go first."

There was no reason to argue; I needed to trust him, like he trusted me. But I questioned whether or not he did right now because of the vision. So if that was true, he'd be pretending, but it was good enough for now. I would later prove to him that the visions were real.

I went back upstairs to gather my bags. The pink blanket was scattered across my bed, hiding under the top of the covers. My firm grip rolled up the fuzzy throw and twirled it into one of my bags. When I packed on vacations, I usually just stuffed the clothes and shoes into any space in the duffel bag. So I did it now, there was no time to fold anything- but don't assume I don't know how to fold, because I do.

"Come on Nikki!" Cameron yelled.

I looked around the room once more to see if I left anything on the floor or bed; my body anxiously running down the stairs to finally look for more clues. It had been a little while seen this whole thing actually started.

The door was left wide open; I looked at the old-dated empty house and raced into the car. I had no idea what to expect; what we would even find out? But we were doing this on our own, to save our best friend. Loading my bag into the backseat, I ran into Cameron. "Watch where you're going." I sarcastically said while pushing him over.

He laughed. "Ouch." Cameron said touching the spot where I hit him. "When did you get so strong?" This time, I think Cameron was being for real. My heart began racing because I didn't know how to respond. I didn't mean to hurt him like that, it was supposed to be a joke.

"Nick, I'm just joking, I'm fine. But damn, you are strong." He opened the front door of the car. My window was rolled down and I put my face through it looking to him.

"Thank you, Cam." I gave a little grin, showing my confident smile.

"Since when do you call him Cam?" Ash interrupted. I was thrown off guard, I hadn't even remembered calling Cameron like that in a while. My cheeks began turning red, so I hid my nervousness.

"Since now. Ash, put up my window I don't wanna look at this ugly face anymore." I said. Cameron's hand dug right into my face unexpectedly. He closed the door and I hopped into the back seat.

I added an unnecessary explanation. "It also means douche, in Nikki's language." What the heck did I just say? That sounded stupid as hell; especially when Ash expressed confusion and Cameron made a sarcastic sigh.

"Nikki, why don't you go to sleep." Ash said lowering his hands as showing me to calm down.

"Alright, I get it. Ugh." I unzipped my bag and picked up the pink blanket; I dropped it over my face suffocating in its trapped like atmosphere. My eyes closed and the blackness haunted me. I forced a memory of my brain and picked at it decoding every little detail. I was on my bed while Cade was on the floor reading her magazines. We were talking about boys and how we were nervous for our first kiss. Cade said she had watched shows with her mom and that it would come naturally. But the thought of kissing someone always was nerve wracking. I tried to replay our conversation over and over again to remember her voice. Anything that could erase the recent sounds that came out of Cade's tortured soul.

"Cade are-" Cameron stopped.

I opened my eyes and tossed the blanket on the other side of the seat. "Nikki are you hungry?" Cameron asked, his cheeks a little red from mistaking my name for a missing girl.

"Yeah, I could eat." I sat up and tightened my seatbelt a little more to firmly grip across my chest. Cameron pulled the car into a Seven Eleven.

"Ok, 10 minutes." He pulled out cash from his pocket and split it between the three of us. I grabbed the 10 dollars and walked into the store. I quickly remembered the amber alert sent out for me so I hid my face lower than usual. My stomach rumbled and I needed something filling. Walking over to the selections of sandwiches, I hoped for a simple one. Maybe a lettuce, cheese and tomato. Thankfully, there was one left and I grabbed it with a sparkling seltzer. I didn't want to lift my head, someone would notice who I was, but I didn't have to. Ash's voice called for Cameron and I could tell I was involved in this signal. We all met at the cash register; the line was not so long. There were about four people in front of us. I was becoming anxious and Ash noticed me tapping my foot on the floor. There were no signs that he wanted me to stop, so I continued doing it until the line finally brought us to the front. If we were checking out together how come he needed to split the money? Right now that thought wasn't important. I kept my head down while the other boys were acting normal. I lifted my head up and turned around to look at Cameron.

A man was behind Cameron chewing on his gum. I made quick eye contact with him and turned around. "Hey, you're that girl." All of the sudden I felt a body move into me, holding me like he was guarding me from the sides.

"Excuse me, we need to go." Ash took the money from our hands and handed it to the lady.

"Nikki Field, you're *her*."

This wasn't good. I couldn't help myself but look at the man who was calling me out on my crime. To my surprise Cameron was the one holding me. I turned around to let my face press on the back of Cameron. The cash register made a noise when money was pulled out. "Let's go." Ash said. He grabbed my hand and my head left the protection of Cameron. I felt like I was in a movie because Cameron's hand took my other arm and they were pulling me out of the store. The man left the line and his voice followed our footsteps to the car. "Hi, I possibly found Nikki Field. She is a the Seven Eleven on 40th." The sound of someone reporting me made my heart beat faster. I looked at Ash who pulled me harder by the arms. The paper bag was dangling from the side of Ash as the food rattled back and forth. They both let go of my arms and I opened the door. My hand skidded across the black car and my feet overlapped each other.

"God." I collected myself and opened the door. The engine roared while I slipped my seat belt over me as fast as possible.

"GO!" Ash shouted hitting the window. I started hearing sirens and saw flashing bright blue and red lights near by. I sat up from my seat still buckled.

"Cameron!" My teeth chattered.

His hands were moving all over the wheel. He turned out of the Seven Eleven parking lot and onto the street. The cars pulled into the store from the other side of the road. I could see them making their way onto our street.

The car pushed forward and I was knocked back down into my seat. A few honks rose my attention that Cameron was probably doing something illegal. We had gone the normal pace as any other car, but tried to cut a few. We passed one light and were stopped at the second. The police cars lined up behind "Pull over." The speaker announced. The red light switched to green and we were once again speeding in the zone, trying to get far away from them as possible.

"This is all my fault." I covered my hands over my face.

No one made any remarks, they were too busy trying to get me out of my mess. If it weren't for them, I don't know what I would do. Right now I needed Cade. A shoulder to lean on and rant about everything that went wrong. Though, it hit me when I realized my pain was nowhere near to Cade's. I turned my head to face the flat window above the trunk. The police cars were right behind us as we were swerving back and forth in front of cars; we went out of our seats as Cameron jolted over the bumps.

"Turn right." Ash said.

Cameron turned the car and went through a red light messing up the intersection. We almost bumped into two other cars and one guy stuck the middle finger out of their window. My usual impulsive response was to curse back, but we were too busy trying to get lost from the cars. After we safely got to the right curb the people in their cars were yelling and we had caused an accident. The police cars were stuck in the middle trying to make their way out of the mess.

"Keep going, we are losing them." I said happily.

The vibe in the car was settling down. We were thirty minutes away from the address; a buzzer exploded through my phone. Another amber alert. What could they have possibly have to say?

Chapter 10

A mber Alert: A female, Nikki Field, has gone missing from State Mental Hospital.

Description: Age 16, Caucasian, dark brown hair, green eyes

Height- 5'6

Weight- 130

License: RJK3506

Black Sudan

With Cameron Sawyer and Ash Gallen

"Cameron!" I whined after seeing this aggravating text. Both boys reacted and Ash checked his phone. "We need to get out of this car, now."

"What? Why?" Cameron said turning left.

"They know what car we are in and that we are with Nikki."

Cameron pulled over into the nearest gas station that was surprisingly right ahead and stopped immediately. He ejected the key and the gas turned off. "What are you doing?" I asked.

"We are getting out of this car." Cameron opened his door, angry. Taking the bag from the back he gave no clear instructions. His face was blank, but underneath the flat surface there was a raging fury. I knew Cameron was mad about this whole situation; his attitude made me want to run away from his sight. Ash was out of the car by my side with the other bag. I gave him a look while Cameron was on his phone. Ash gave me a sly smile and my body tingled with a longing to kiss him.

"We are going to get an uber." Cameron said. Was he crazy? Where would we put our car? The idea of ditching it was insane. What would his mother say after finding his car in the middle of nowhere?

"What about your car?" I asked.

"What about it?" Cameron didn't laugh or show any act of sadness. I was confused by his sudden change in demeanor. I slipped my hand under Ash's and walked into the gas station.

"Where are you guys going?"

"Will wait for the uber in the store." Ash turned around and waved for Cameron to come along. He rolled his eyes and I lay my head down on Ash's shoulder. His soft sweatshirt made me want to doze off and curl up in bed. Ash opened the door and let go of my hand. "Want to get something?"

"Gum." I made a weird expression and Ash laughed. He took three dollars out of his pocket and picked out my favorite kind. Number 5. He pointed to the door and I inferred he wanted me to stay there so no one would catch me again.

About two minutes later, while I was standing looking outside to see Cameron on his phone, I felt two hands on my shoulders.

"That was supposed to scare you." Ash said sarcastically frustrated.

"Trust me, it's gonna take a lot more than that." I sighed and peeled off the wrapper. The gum went into my mouth and the taste of freshness was exactly what I needed.

"Sorry, that was stupid."

"It's okay, Ash. I know you were only trying to cheer me up."

Ash moved in closer and kissed me on the cheek. His lips shocked me and warmness swept through my cold body. His phone buzzed. "It's here, let's go." Taking initiative, Ash took my arm and dragged me to the uber car.

"Get in." He gently pushed me into car with him and Cameron following.

I kept my face dug in Ash's body. "Where to?" The cab driver asked; his voice static and old. The smell of the car reminded me of the elderly. It was familiar from visiting my grandmother, I had nothing against it, It was kind of comforting once in awhile.

"34 Baker street." Cameron said stuffing the bags under the chair in front of him.

"Alright, they are closing soon."

What did he mean by *they*?

"What do you-?"

"Ok, strap your seatbelts, and we'll be off." Cameron was interrupted before he could finish his sentence. We buckled our seatbelts and the noise of the car settled down as we got closer to the address.

A little while after, maybe 30 minutes or so, we arrived at 34 Baker Street. "Get out of the car, Nikki." Cameron said taking his money and handing it to the driver.

"Don't speak to her that way." The driver remarkably added.

He shot me an embarrassed expression. " It's a lot more complicated, sir."

He laughed. "Nothing warrants to talk to a woman like that, son. No matter how complicated."

The advice coming out of the driver's mouth was perplexing, but sort of right. Why did Cameron have the authority to tell me what to do? But I kind of liked it when he did; he sounded manly and bad. That was my type.

He closed the car door and looked at me.

"It's ok Cam, I know you could never have the power to talk to me like that." I flipped my hair into his face.

"Ok Nick, we get it. Sorry I won't be *so* demanding." He rounded the word "so" which I was happy about. We could still quarrel and enjoy our practical jokes.

"Are you sure this is right?" Ash said plugging the address into his phone. It was weird to think they hadn't done that earlier.

"Yeah it says it."

"Huh, It's a library." Ash said walking forward to the big sign that red: "Books of the Beginning"

The sign was sculpted into a sideways diamond that was wooden brown with silver lettering. It stood about 6 feet tall and the large letters could be seen back onto the road. The opening of the library was wide; an entrance with automatic doors that we walked in. From the beginning the display of books was enormous. They were organized so evenly; book shelves started from the left all the way to the right. But before you got to the books two desks were planted in front.

"Well, what do we do now?" Ash said turning to the both of us who were still stuck staring at the place. I could see stairs built at the end of the right wing that swirled up onto the second level. A kid's room was built up there and little children were laughing playing with blocks. I had an urge to smile, but Ash's continuous questions broke me out of that feeling.

"Well, we know the app was some sort of thing for tutoring."

"What if we looked it up online?" I said finally having a good idea.

The section of computers was a little before the staircase, closer to the window. There were two desks for the stack of computers that lay across the counters. Cameron sat down and googled "tutoring apps."

A list of sites popped up onto the page; Cameron moved the clicker to the first one. The opening of the site read "Tutoring Now Available With A Button Away."

"Was this the one?" Cameron turned around to me with a fussy look.

"I-I don't remember." I tried to recall what the app was before talking to the user. My brain was shutting down every time I needed to think really hard. It was enough already comprehending what I've gone through. "What if you look up the user?"

"Do it. User504." The keyboard clicked and I was nervous to see if there was a way of contact. Cameron pressed on the search button and around four usernames popped up. The first one was exactly the same; he clicked on it and it worked.

"What are we gonna say?" Ash said pulling up a chair. I sat on his lap but moved over to let Ash's head peak through.

"Say hi, I heard from a friend you are a really good tutor."

Cameron typed the same sentence and sent it without

even checking over his spelling. My foot tapped again on the carpeted floor and Ash touched my arm. I was impatient at this point and my temperature was heating up.

"He isn't responding!"

"How do you know it's a he?" Ash asked.

"*It* was flirting with Cade." I looked behind to see Ash's face in shock. I recognized the expression. He was processing the mess he was in and what happened to his friend.

We waited around 10 minutes looking up other sites, but there were no other matches for the right user. "Well, what are we gonna do now?"

"Obviously Cade was here and used the tutor. Maybe we should see if there are any other 34 Baker Streets that aren't a library- not making it obvious when she was." I gulped. "Taken."

"Ok, good idea. I'll get another uber."

Ash put the chair back while Cameron slid his in. He logged out of the site and cleared the history which was a good idea. Anyone could find that and see what we said.

We made our way to the two exits when I came across a bulletin board. It was bright with the alphabet and encouraging quotes. I remembered the one at our school, where all the writing and drawings were hung up. Ours was way bigger than this, but I began to miss my school. Hell, I never knew I would say this, but I miss my old life.

"What is it?" Cameron came back. He looked at my face that was covered in slow water. His dull expression suddenly changed to his sensitive one. I only saw this one a few times; whenever Cade hurt herself or something happened and they were talking; I could see his face. I never knew he would do it to me.

"Nick."

God. His voice, his whole body was calling me. I leaped for a hug and my shoulder dug into his. My eyes cried and I visioned me reuniting with Cade. Why was God doing this to me? I didn't even believe in one, but sure the world couldn't be like this.

I looked up and saw Ash sitting on the bench outside. He wasn't looking so I took advantage of this moment. I hugged him tighter, and he hugged me back even tighter. I smiled and let go.

"It reminded me of school." I said.

'Trust me, we are all better off not being there." He laughed. "We are all missing it."

His words suddenly spiraled downward as I zoomed in on advertisements of tutoring. There was a list of names signed up on a chart below the kid friendly greets "Look, Cameron." I tugged his white shirt closer to where I was looking.

The list read 7 names:

Elijah Calls

Ryan Lib

Daniel Gross

Tanner Rid

Sebastian D

Freddie Dass

"We should take this." Cameron said reaching for the paper.

"What if people notice it's gone?"

"Do you not get it? This is it Nikki. If we get this and show it to my mom, there might be a chance to save Cade"

"You're right. Let's go." I lead the two of us out the door.

"What is that?" Ash looked at Cameron's hand.

"Something that is going to help save Cade."

The uber car pulled up and we hopped in. "Wait, where are our bags?"

"Shoot. Hold on." Cameron went back inside.

"He put them by the desk." Ash said. Cameron came back with the bags and sat in the front seat.

"What address?" The driver asked.

"We are going to the police station."

"Are you sure your mom is there?" I asked.

Cameron turned his head around. "Yeah, I mean I assume so."

We turned out of the driveway. The tears were still making their way onto my lap so I quickly rubbed them off before anyone noticed. The station was around 10 minutes away so I rested my head on Cameron- I mean Ash. He always had the softest shoulders so whenever we were watching a movie I would cuddle with him. In the middle of movies, he would kiss my cheeks and rub my hair.

I tried to find my happy place within these minutes. Anything that could distract me from figuring out if it was humanly possible to solve a murder, let alone find the one who was "murdered."

The memory of the four of us wiped away the pain. We were planning to go into town and graffiti something on a bench. I was the one to come up with the image, but nothing had come to me that day. I was always interested in that dark, edgy art. Whenever I went into the city, I would look for graffiti works. Either names or weird sketches would be drawn across the bridges or buildings. They caught my attention like that. Nobody really appreciated the meanings behind this stuff. These artists were coming from a place of sadness, curiosity or happiness. Not even that, but they had something to tell the world. Don't get me wrong, I know it's illegal. But that makes it much cooler. These people are willing to break the law to show their voice. I loved it so much, that I had an idea to do that.

At first everyone agreed and thought it would be cool, but later Cameron said he didn't want to get in any trouble. I told Ash to convince him to join us, and Cameron caved. It was so exciting being able to do this. The thing I was confused about is how we were going to get the paint. I couldn't tell my mom about it; out of all of us, my mom was the sanest. Cade had the idea to steal the paint from the store. In the beginning, I was so nervous because I was really bad at lying, but Cade wasn't. So she broke up a plan and told us about it the night before. We were going to do it on a Friday night at the King Kullen nearby.

Cade said we would walk in pairs. I would go with Ash and Cade would go with Cameron. She told us Ash would be checking out the sports stuff, while I went with Cade to find the paint. Cameron would be up top by the register and pretend to look at stuff to buy. Cade told me to tell Ash when we got everything, so I did. We got all the spray cans in colors, black, white and blue.

Ash then whistled over to Cameron who nodded. Cade put the paint in her bags and we walked together to look at products closer to the cash register. Ash went over with a football in his hands to Cameron who took a pack of gum. They lined up at the cash register and Cade and I pretended to be looking around. "Line 4." The announcement said. The boys walked up together and paid; while Cade and I changed to the other side to look at the crafts.

"Thank you." Ash said smiling walking away with the bag.

We all met up and walked out together; the buzzer went off, which we knew was going to happen. Neither Cade nor I had a worried face, we prepared for this. One of the clerks came over to us and checked their bags. We sat on the bench before the two opening doors waiting for our plan to work. The shuffling of the hands in the bags made my stomach twirl. We were so close to getting away with it. "Ok, must have been a false alarm." The women announced into her walkie-talkie I took a breath and lay my head on Cade's shoulders who laughed.

The boys thanked the clerk and walked out of the store. We followed, having trouble containing our excitement. "I told you. " Cade said. She slightly showed the paint to the boys.

"Ok, let's go. I know what we are going to paint." I took the bag from Cade and ran over to the car.

"What are we going to draw?" Cameron asked looking through the bag.

"Superman sign." I said with confidence and a hint of a pose.

"What the hell?" Ash said laughing and turning out of the driveway. My sudden lift of happiness had changed from a big plump grape to a shriveled raisin.

"It was our first double date movie." Cade said.

I looked at her and mouthed, I love you. She smiled and we lay our heads on the window looking at the rain pouring down.

"Where are we gonna even paint it?" Cameron asked.

I changed my mind, not the bench anymore. "The locker rooms."

The boys laughed and Cade commented how that was a cool idea.

"No, I like it Nick." Cameron said pretending to spray the can.

"Yeah, me too." Ash said.

Whether or not they were joking, I was excited to do it. Finally, I was going to make my mark and share my voice, even though it was a just a symbol.

"Ok, we are here." I awoke off of Ash's shoulder.

I don't know why I remembered the memory so well. Maybe because we all connected and had fun. We never got caught and could share the thrill of the experience.

We got out of the car and arrived at the station.

"Cameron, this isn't gonna be good."

Before long the cops came out with their guns and handcuffs. "Stay down." They said to me. I never knew what it felt like to be targeted by a lethal weapon. It was an out of body experience to know an option was to kill me if we didn't cooperate.

"Guys, what is happening here?" The voice sounded familiar. I could only see blonde hair in the view coming into the crowd of officers.

"Cam!" My voice trembling as his mother was coming closer to seeing it was us.

"I got it, don't worry." He said with relaxed hands.

"Now, what is?" She cocked her head at us. "Cameron?" Her voice cracking. She sprinted towards him for a hug.

"Mom, I'm fine. Really."

"Nikki? Where have you guys been?" Her voice raised. Then she turned around and waved the guns down. The men slowly retreated their weapons and I began to feel more comfortable.

"Ms. Sawyer." I said.

"Nikki, we must get you back to the hospital and let your parents know where you are. They are worried sick. This is not good."

"Cameron!" I agitatedly said trying not to sound loud.

"Mom, Wait. Give us five minutes and we will explain everything." He stopped. She let go of my arm. "Please." He said, this time it was for real. Like he wanted her to listen more than anything.

Her hesitation was easy to see. The biting of her lip made it harder to stand still- I wanted to get on with it.

"Fine. Come with me." I walked back and somehow fell into the middle of Ash and Cameron. Alison seemed to forget Ash was behind the two of us.

We entered the police office and everyone became quiet. All eyes were on us while we shamefully walked into his mother's office. Alison's office was in the corner on the other side of the station. Although the door was glass, curtains covered the scene to block the conversation. Alison went to chair having a stiff posture and stern face. I was hoping Cameron knew what to say.

"Talk Cameron." Alison said, but somehow she was questioning him and speaking like he wasn't her son.

"Well-."

"Cameron, I am not in the mood for games."

"Cade is still alive." I blurted out.

God, I have a serious problem.

"Honey, I think you need to go back-."

"Mom, just frickin listen to her." Cameron sat up and yelled. His tone stunned me and I felt out of place. I would get these feelings sometimes like I wasn't living. To comprehend, I was who I was, what I looked like; how I'm breathing. It would hit me hard and when Cameron yelled and stood up to his mother, I felt the feeling.

Alison's eyes widened. The time finally came for her to accept Cameron was an adult and that he had something to say.

"What do you mean by that, Nikki?"

"I will get to that later." I said reaching into my bag. "Here is a list of names we found at the library."

"What is this for?" Alison took it out of my hands and read it over.

"We were here, we went through Cade's phone." I didn't know whether to leave that part out, but it was done and over with and I needed to accept Cameron's reaction.

She cocked her head up and looked at me. "Nikki, do you know that is illegal?"

"She wasn't the only one, Mom." Cameron said putting his head down.

"Cameron? Why?"

"Because- my friend is alive."

"I will deal with this later, just tell me what happened."

"Well, Cade was on an app for tutoring. And the one we think took her, was flirting with her. Being all weird and stuff."

Alison took her time to think. She kept tapping the desk. "We have confirmation that its Cade's body."

"It's not her, mom." Cameron said.

"Are you sure it is? Did they do a DNA check?" I was sure to make my point clear. There must be something I could do to convince this was all wrong. If only Cade was here right now to help me like she did with Ash. Alison looked at her computer and typed quickly. I was fidgeting with my hands trying to distract myself from the silence. The keyboard clicked and clicked and I grew more impatient.

"An officer sent an email to all of us saying he checked the DNA."

"Do you know who?"

"I'm not allowed to share that information."

"There must be some sort of explanation- I just don't think it's possible for Cade to be alive, I mean there is evidence of Cade's body according to one of my partners."

This wasn't right. We couldn't get anywhere until Alison believed us. I closed my eyes.

"What is she doing?" Alison asked confused.

I got up from my chair and started walking around the room. My eyes half open to know where I was going, but once I knew the space I shut them. "Come on Cade, come on."

All I saw was darkness. I tried thinking about memories with Cade. Maybe if I focused on her I could control the visions. But I realized it didn't work like that, only Cade had that ability.

"Cameron, what is going on?"

"Mom, just wait." Cameron said in the background.

"Cade, come on. Help me." It sounded so selfish to say

that. After all, she could be dead right now, but the string was still there so maybe she wasn't. A few seconds later while my eyes were shut and spiraling into the black light, Cade appeared.

"Cade!"

"I don't have time, Nick.

"She doesn't believe me."

Cade looked at her arms, long streaks of blood covered her tan skin. A knife was next to her dripping drops of blood onto the floor.

"Crap." I said. For the knife was only a small weapon that would be used on Cade's body.

"What is it, Nikki?" Cameron asked.

I gulped. "She has-cuts." I stared at her existence, almost like a spirit about to vanish. *Don't go* I wanted to say. I wanted to tell her everything was fine, she didn't need to die. But I had no idea what she was going through.

"What-how?" I heard a soft whisper from Alison.

"Cade, Just something." I begged.

"Look for the DNA on the charts, it isn't there. Also Alison cheated on Cameron's father."

My mouth dropped. Out of my chest. Out of my heart. How would Cade know this? Could she have walked in on a conversation? I didn't know what I was going to say when Cameron asked the question, "What did she say?"

I sat back down on my chair tapping my foot on the floor. My eyes spaced as a hand rubbed my back shoulder. "Check the DNA, now." What I said wasn't directly to Alison, just anybody who could hear and help me. Help Cade and me from falling apart.

"An officer did the check, it's done."

I slammed my foot onto the floor and grabbed the front of Alison's desk. I had no idea what Cameron or Ash saw in me. Either a psycho chick or a loyal best friend, " Check the god-damn DNA." I had a tendency to act rude towards adults. It was a habit of mine ever since I was able to form sentences. I was never one to agree with a teacher's point. That's when I really defied the laws of "respecting teachers." I had never meant it in a bad way, I just told it as I saw it, and not all teachers want to be outed by a kid with no life experience.

"Nikki, calm down. I will."

I took a breath and looked at Cameron, whose cheeks were flushed. My heart was beating so loudly and sweat was forming on my arms and head.

"This is not right." Alison took a better look at the screen. I got up from my chair and moved onto her side. She looked at me, but didn't say anything.

"There is nothing on here. I don't get it." Alison wiped her face and sat up from her black swiveling chair.

"Where are you going?" Ash asked. I forgot he was here. The whole time Ash was quiet on the couch; I wonder what he thought of me now, since my almost break down.

"I'm looking into the records, there must be a mistake." Alison looked through the evidence files following in alphabetical order. The way she looked for the papers, made me think I was getting under her skin.

She pulled out the paper that was filed nicely in a grey folder. "Cade's Case" it read on the front. My body shook with anticipation. Knowing they must have screwed up made me angry;. there was no way there could be DNA evidence.

"This is unbelievable." Alison said combing her fingers through her hair.

"What?" Cameron asked.

"I know it was ordered, we always order DNA evidence when there is a burned body. But there are no results confirming it was Cade Murphy's."

"I told you." I said to Alison, trying to hide my frustration.

"How did you know that?"

Cameron jumped in, saving me once again. "She can see Cade, and now she can literally have visions."

"And Cade told me to look at the DNA." I kept the other part out for now. I had to fully process what Cade told me. If Cameron found out his mother cheated on his father, their whole family would be broken. Cameron was sensitive, especially when it came to family problems. He was a Cancer, they are known for being attached to family and moody. I would hate to see this ruin his life.

"When did this start happening?" Alison asked. Her face was in awe.

"Right after she died." I said. This feeling was familiar. It was honesty and trust. The same as when Cameron found out, then Ash. It was good to know people were believing me, but I know it killed Cade on the inside to give me this information. She was in such pain, and I would hate to know how much effort it took to communicate with me.

"Do you believe us? Cameron asked. "I have a feeling we can get the guy."

"I know there are some suspects here, my mom told me while I was at the hospital. We can help." I said.

There were no words to truly express Alison's face. Maybe

it was between confusion, sadness and awe. A tear rolled down her eyes and I knew she was upset. After all, Cade was Cameron's girlfriend and they were all close.

"This just doesn't make sense- I have to call your mother."

"No. Stop." My hands stopped her before she reached for her phone.

"Mom. How could you?" Cameron said disgusted. We finally got Alison to listen to us, but she was going to blow it for a phone call.

"Honey, this is the right thing. We need to help Nikki."

My hands gave up. This was useless trying to explain to someone my "power." I sat back down in the chair and the water started pouring. Ash came over to me and started rubbing my back. He was quiet the whole time and I was shocked when he said something. "Listen, I get it. It's crazy. I didn't believe Nikki at first. That was a mistake. But I can put my life on the line and say that Cade's still alive and Nikki is telling the truth." Ash was getting hotter and nicer by the second. My feelings mixed as I thought about Cameron. They both were sticking up for me and in the end I felt like It would just blow up in my face.

"Mom, please just let us try. Give us a day."

"A *day*." I could see Alison was trying to suppress a smile.

I knew deep down somewhere she believed me. But that was all I needed for now. There was no way I was going to let her think I was living a lie, not her, not anyone.

Chapter 11

Alison was nice enough to let the three of us sleep at her house. Calls were racing on the phones before we left the station and she told me my mom asked if they found anything. Alison lied and said she would keep looking for me, but guaranteed I was fine. The bed was uneven and made my back hurt more than usual. The dull ache eventually turned to needles pointing into my fragile body. We all slept in one room after Alison said it was alright to be separated. I told her I was fine, but Cameron and Ash insisted to be with me. I sat up from the bed and looked to see the boys rolled over on their backs. They had slept on blowups that flattened almost to the floor. I never liked sleeping on those things, even when I was with Cade I would always complain. So from then on, Cade said I could sleep in her bed. That was something I was grateful for.

I looked at the alarm clock next to me.

8 am.

The two pillows next to me were thrown at the boys beds. One of the pillows hit Cameron in the face and the other hit Ash's body. "Ah." I bit my lip cause I threw them a little too hard.

Ash's body moved and Cameron moaned. I laughed and threw another pillow at Cameron. This time it hit his body and he twisted to the other side. Ash's eyes started to open and I cracked my neck side to side. My muscles loosened and I took a minute to relax and massage the back of it.

"Why did you hit me?" Ash whispered.

"Because, we are leaving soon."

"Alison told us she would take us." Ash responded.

"I know." I smiled and took off the covers. My shorts were black with two white strips on the side. They rolled past my upper thigh; part of my butt cheek was standing out, but I didn't mind. The soft cotton material was easy to sleep with. I hated being in pants and sweatshirt at night; under all the covers and blankets it felt like a sauna.

I crawled softly to Cameron's blow up while Ash stretched his arms. I made sure to keep my legs out of reach from his body. My attempt was to wake Cameron up by annoying him. He was never the type of guy to get up early, more like a late bird. I would text him around 9 in the morning and he would never respond. He and Cade were similar when it came to small things like that. For example, they liked the same ice cream flavor with the same kind of sprinkles, they both loved the color green and watching basketball. Cameron use to get tickets since his uncle was a manager of one team. He always took Cade and never really asked me, I didn't say anything because it would look weird in front of Cade, I assumed.

"Cameron." I took him.

My hand was wrapped around his muscular arm. I pulled his body to flip over, but his body weight was heavier than I expected. He sniffed his nose and unwrapped his arm to wipe it. I looked away and laughed while Ash was doing the same thing. He mouthed to me to poke him, so I took my tiny finger and started tapping him on the head. I didn't know if I was being too hard because I saw the impression on his forehead.

"Wha-?" Cameron yawned and fully flipped over with his

head facing on the ceiling. I jumped on him and my legs spread across on both sides. His eyes were open and he smiled. "Hi Cade." Everything in the world just stopped. I had felt stupid and foolish to try to act silly. I didn't know where I was going with this, it wasn't meant to be some sort of flirtatious move. I looked halfway behind me and saw Ash taking his shirt off to change. Did he see what I did? Did he mind? My heart was pulling me in different directions and I could see this ending would not be good. I couldn't think like this, I needed to focus on what was most important: Cade.

I got off him and went over to my small navy bag. I rubbed the edges of the nylon and grinded my teeth. "Nikki, I'm sorry. I don't know why I said that."

A tear dropped from my eye, I was certainly over-reacting. "It's okay, Cam." I turned to face him and gave a gentle smile.

I picked up the bag and walked into the bathroom. The bag plopped onto the toilet seat and my eyes caught the mirror. The bathroom was spacious. White shapes covered the middle part of the wall. The circles tightened and made their way across the center of the whole bathroom. The light features dazzled on two opposite sides of the mirror making me see blue spots as I looked away. I chased my way down to the sink that was circled. The silver faucet stood sparkly clean and I wiped the tip of it, picking up some water. It was a while since I looked at myself in the mirror, nothing looked drastically different to me.

Plain old Nikki.

No- plain old Cade- according to Cameron.

I headed back to the room with my dirty clothes smushed into my bag. The zipper was caught on a piece of clothing, but I was too lazy to do anything about it. The boys were changed by the time I got back and their beds were tightly made. "Ready to go?" I asked.

"Aren't we going to wait for my mom?" Cameron asked walking towards me.

"No, I wanna go before she comes back. I wanted prove to her that I knew what I was doing." I turned around and walked to the staircase. The footsteps of Ash and Cameron followed behind me as I ran down the stairs.

"Want anything to eat?" Ash said making his way into the kitchen.

"Nah, just want to get going."

Cameron came out of the kitchen with an orange in his hand. The sides were slightly peeled off and their trail followed his steps. "Can we go please?" I moaned in a whiny voice and regretted it once the words left my mouth. I quickly looked away and shut the door behind me to erase my tone because I didn't want to hear their response. When It came to criticism, I was always defensive. It was a characteristic I was naturally born with. I hoped I had gotten better since I was little, but that didn't mean there were times where I was blankly rude.

The car clicked and I assumed the doors were open. I pushed my bag into the front of the car seat and waited for the boys to come out. The hot sticky car made me regret the choice to wear leggings, but it was all I had with me. The police had gotten the car back from where we left it after our return was announced. Thankfully, no one stole it and it was left in one piece. I took the knob back onto the chair and let it press backward. The boys were nowhere in sight and I began to feel annoyed and pissed. First, I was cranky because I didn't eat anything. And I know Ash asked me, but there was no time to waste. I rolled the car window down and started calling out for Ash and Cameron. I could see my breath leave my mouth as the cold froze my nose and lips.

"We need to find Cade." I whispered to myself. It was some sort of motivation to keep telling myself she was alive. There was no point to get discouraged after all I've seen from her. It still hurt me that nobody truly knew how I felt on the inside. I got up to the front of the car and started honking the horn. The pressure of the sound would hopefully be enough to get the boys out of the house.

"Nikki."

I jumped out from the rest between the two chairs and looked to the back of me. Cade was lying down looking up at the car ceiling. Her legs bruised and patched a pattern on the upper thighs. She was still in her shorts and top; the feeling shivered through my body.

"Cade!" I got up and planned to go over and help. But my body started hurting. Right then and there I felt a sharp knife penetrate my upper right rib. My hands was placed on it as I imagined the blood dripping down. But there was no blood, only the feeling of stabbing pain suffocating me under it's reign of red.

My breaths were shorter and my voice began to lower. "Cade, what are you doing?" It sounded like I was blaming her for something. Was she making me feel this way?

"Nikki. Help me." Cade's head turned to me and her left eye was black and blue. The edges of the skin were peeled off and my heart ached.

"Owe." Then my right eye was hurting. The dull feeling of it was vibrating and giving me a migraine. Her hand was over the same place that was hurting me. I lifted my shirt up to see evidence of how much my body hurt, but again, nothing. I sunk on the floor of the car because the knife still stuck wounds in my skin.

"Cade, help." I looked to the car and saw Cameron and Ash coming down. My voice was weak and I couldn't make a big enough sound to tell them to run. My legs were shaking and I imagined the bruised spots covering my legs. My leggings disappeared and only the shorts were noticeable from my view.

"What is happening, Cade?" My rib was screaming at me.

"I'm sorry, Nikki."

She looked up to the ceiling and disappeared.

"Nikki!" Ash was the one who spotted me first. I couldn't see Cameron, but Ash turned around and yelled something after that.

There was no time for me. I realized I was Cade. Well, I was *In* her.

Chapter 12

"She's waking up." A fuzzy noise in the background said. The monitor beeping was hard to hear if my vitals were normal or not. High-pitched and short, they repeated every two seconds. I counted the beating. My eyes were wandering to check my surroundings. There were two people on opposite sides; a tall blonde nurse with her board in her hands and an older male feeling my feet.

"Hi, Nikki." The male's voice was old and masculine. It kind of reminded me of Derek Shepherd from Grey's Anatomy. His hair was fluffed to the side and his facial hair was buzzed slightly.

"Where am I?" I felt my rib because the memory of it hurting interrupted my questions.

"Why are you feeling your rib?" He looked at the other nurse and I quickly dragged my hand away from it.

"Nothing." I coughed and asked why he was touching my feet.

"I want to see if you have any numbness." His prints marked my bottom and top feet. The pressure was the same, nothing different than before.

"Why am I here?" I said after realizing it was a hospital, the mint curtains and bed clued me in.

"Two boys brought you here. They said they found you passed out in the car."

I wrinkled my nose and looked at him. His bright watch

was glazed with a navy wrap and the outer core sparkled with silver jewels.

"Where are they?"

"In the waiting room. But first I would like to ask you some questions." He nodded at the nurse who left the room.

"I am not talking to anyone unless I see them."

"I knew you were going to say that." He smiled. "Also, I'm Dr. Brick."

Wow, even a hot name too. God, what the heck was I saying?

"Nurse Taylor went to go get them."

I crossed my hands and slouched on the two pillows behind me. They weren't soft like my other ones. I missed the feeling of my bed; the way I felt when I got in, all wrapped up.

"I will be back to talk to you."

Dr. Brick walked out of the room and closed the curtains behind me. I tapped my feet together and started singing Moana. "I wish, I could be the perfect daughter." Something inside of me hoped Cade would sing and finish the rest.

A couple minutes later Ash and Cameron came in speed walking to the other sides of me. "Are you okay?" Ash said rubbing my leg. I flashed the memory of my shorts and bruised legs.

"Yeah. I think so."

"What happened?" Cameron asked sitting on the chair.

"I remember everything. I was in the car waiting for you guys and then I saw Cade. She was like- like dead. Her body was lying down on the back seat and she wasn't moving. All of the sudden my rib started to hurt, then my eye."

"What do you think it could be?" Ash asked.

"I think- I was in Cade. Or more like I could feel what she was feeling. But either way, it's freaky as hell."

"I don't get how all these things are happening." Cameron scratched his head and wiped his face with his hands.

"I know. Especially me."

"Well, to answer the second part- because you are her best friend? And the rest I have no freaking idea." Ash said laughing.

Ash did have a point. There was no other bond like ours and I knew why it was me. But Cameron's questions were valid. However, I knew there was no explanation to explain why this was all happening, and how.

"Whatever, but listen. I can't tell them I passed out because I felt my dead friend's pain, so we need your mom to help."

"I kind of already told her we are here."

"What did she say?"

"She was really worried, but I told her that you would talk to her."

"OK good. Dr. Brick is going to ask me questions- I need her here."

"Oh, and also- your parents are coming. I mean since they found out we returned."

"What?!"

"My mom tried to keep them from knowing as long as possible, but it was time."

"I guess." There was no point to argue. What was done, was done. My mom would soon be here, yelling at me for my careless behavior. Alison would soon lose her smidge of trust because her interpretation could have been "faking it." The doctor was gonna come back and ask me all sorts of questions. I needed to think of something- I needed Alison. I needed an excuse.

※

A few minutes passed and the doctor came in with a clipboard of files. "Hi boys, I'm gonna have to ask you to go."

The nurse came and opened the curtains to show them the way out. "They aren't going anywhere. I'm waiting for someone."

"Nikki this is private-."

"I told you, I'm not answering anything."

The boys smiled and crossed their arms; it was timed perfectly.

"I'm here!" A voice came through the curtains. Alison was in her uniform and had her gun at her hip. I don't know why, but that's where my eyes leaped to first.

"And who are you?" The doctor cocked his head and made a suspicious expression.

"I'm the police." Alison's tone shifted while she stuck out her badge. I smiled and laughed inside of me because that was a hell of a move. The boys looked at each other, then me. I sighed from relief that I wasn't going to be alone.

"Alright, well. I am going to continue with questions."

"Sounds alright to me, Doctor." Alison made her way over to my bed. Unexpectedly, she placed her hand over my lower right leg.

"What is the last thing you remember?"

"I was waiting in the car for Cameron and Ash."

Everything was going well so far. "Did you feel anything waking up?"

"No."

"So you were in the car when you started ; feel dizzy?"

"Yes."

The doctor was scribbling his little notes onto my file.

"Why were you touching your rib before?"

That one had got me. I glanced at Cameron from the corner of my eye, trying to prolong my answer.

"Come on honey- just answer."

I didn't know if Alison was being serious or trying to tell me not to be suspicious of his question.

"I hurt it a while ago, so the memory of feeling dizzy reminded me of that."

"Did you ever come into the hospital for it?"

"No, I was messing around with some friends of mine and got tripped, fell on my rib."

"Alright. Well it seems I have all the information I need." Dr. Brick closed the folder and snapped the pen closed.

He walked through the curtains and his cologne reminded me of Ash's. "What is going on?" Alison lifted her hand and looked at me. I guess that whole scene was to get the doctor off our backs.

"This is gonna sound crazy." Cameron said standing up. Alison turned around and lifted up her hands.

"Well?"

"Make sure the curtains are closed."

Ash got up and shut them more. He peeked his head outside and nodded for me to continue. "I was in the car, I saw Cade again."

"Did she tell you anything?"

"No- but I felt her pain. Like I was her for a second."

"This is so fricken weird." Alison chuckled nervously.

"I know. It hurt so badly." I looked at my body. The leggings stirred my memory and the image of blood stirred my stomach.

"What do we do now?" Ash asked.

"Ahh." I touched my head that started beating like a drum. My ears were ringing and my head was flooding with noise.

"Close your eyes!" Cade's spirit appeared to the left of me.

"Cade!" Cameron yelled.

All of their heads turned, but my eyes were forced shut. In the background I could hear Cameron calling my name and hands touching my hands. I tried to open my eyes, but they were glued.

I didn't fight it anymore so I started to breathe slowly and lowered my hands. "Nikki, go to the station. He is going to get away."

"Who is?" Was it her kidnapper?

"Just go!" My eyes popped open and Cade's spirit was gone when I looked over.

"What the hell just happened?" Alison asked.

I took the patch off my arm connecting to a wire that was injecting fluids in my body. "We need to go to the station, Alison. Cade said."

"This is insane. What just happened?"

"I don't know!" I yelled. "But Cade needs us." I pleaded.

"Alright, this is just so crazy." Alison took out her keys and led the way.

"What about the doctor?" Ash asked.

"I will deal with that." Alison said. "But your parents are coming soon, Nikki."

"Please convince them that I need to be with you."

"Go into the car- I will do the rest."

I smiled at Alison, this was it. We were going to find Cade.

We waited around 10 minutes in the car. "What is taking her so long?" I honked the horn.

"Nikki, relax. She is coming."

"Sorry, I'm just worried."

"Why?" Cameron asked.

Ash and I shot him a look. "Oh, I know. But is there something else?"

"Cade said something about not letting him get away."

"What does that mean?"

"I don't know. But I need to go." I honked the horn again.

Alison jogged down the stairs. "Did it."

"What about my parents?"

"I said you are fine, but that they are gonna need to trust me. I said I would tell them everything."

"What!? No, you can't."

"Nikki, I'm not actually going to. I just needed to say that."

"How do they feel about us skipping school?" Cameron asked.

"Your mom will take care of it. As for Ash, I will call your mom later, so don't worry. But Cameron, you are going to need to help us."

Cameron looked at me and smiled. "Thanks mom."

"Now, let's go catch that son of a bitch." Alison said aggressively.

"Mom!" Cameron laughed, but I knew he didn't care.

"What?"

"Nothing, Alison." I rolled my eyes at Cameron. "Just go."

Chapter 13

"Ok listen. A few rules before we go in." Alison stopped us before we entered the door.

"No talking. If you have something to say, tap me and whisper."

"Ok, that's not so hard." I said.

"Do not give them any looks."

What the heck does that mean? I didn't monitor my facial expression. Though, occasionally Ash and Cameron told me I had a resting bitch face.

"Ok, we get it." Cameron said.

We followed Alison past the hallway to a lower level. I've never seen this part of it before. The corner turned downward following a curved path. The stairs were the same kind of hard brown wood and the textured faded walls ran throughout the station. I let Cameron go in front of me, and Ash stayed put in the back.

We walked past a thick black door. My stomach was churning; what if they knew who I was? What if there was someway I could be captured next? There was no way to predict what would happen. I snuck in closer to Cameron, reaching for his hand. But he slipped away before our hands could meet. Then Ash came behind me and grabbed my hand. That was bold, and exactly what I needed. He kissed me on the head and my heart leaped. My body felt warm and tingly. One thing I wanted to do right now was be alone with him, in my room lying on each other.

Cameron turned around and I looked the other way; I wanted him to know what he was missing. He didn't even tell me how we felt after the kiss, nor did I. But all I knew was I was caught in this terrible love triangle. Full of confusion and mystery of where I would go next.

"Ok, remember what I said." Alison stepped into the dark room. It's vibe was unusual and depressing. I held onto Ash's arm tighter; more nervous as I slowly entered this new atmosphere.

"What are those kids doing down here?" An officer said; his beard shaved unevenly and his bright green eyes speaking uncertainty.

"They are with me, James."

He uncrossed his hands and rolled his eyes; I was left with nothing to say or feel.

"Make it quick." James strolled away with his stiff posture. I looked at Alison for approval to continue going. She smiled and motioned me to walk straight ahead.

A big glass wall was across the hallway from where we were. It was connected by a thin strip that only a row of people could fit into. The glass window was trapping the suspects; you have no idea how much I wanted to go in there and knock the shit out of them.

"Nikki, look carefully."

I scanned across the men. They were lined up from tallest to shortest; dressing like they were homeless. The tallest stood out because of the scar on his cheek. It curved like a fish hook touching the end of his jawline. I scrolled down to the end where the shortest one had a tattoo. It looked like a dragon breathing fire; I wanted the fire to kill him.

"Do you see anything?" Ash said rubbing my hand.

I let go of his gentle touch, "Wait, hold on." I walked closer to the tube. My eyes torched through the burning the light the criminals left behind.

I closed my eyes; shutting them tight. "Can you give us a few minutes alone?" Alison turned to James.

"You have five minutes."

"Thank you, James."

I could tell she was playing friendly, but deep down she wanted to take him out. But that was not the way police officers treated each other, especially when children were present.

I waited for the door to shut and it was the four of us and a column of criminals. They were taken from the list, and Cade's tutors from the past. If there was any potential of one of them being the criminal, then I really needed to get my head straight.

I closed my eyes and let my hands slip onto the glass window. A guard was on the other side making sure none of them broke free or got wound up. "What are you doing?" Alison asked. Her voice felt closer, I assumed she walked to me.

"Mom." I heard Cameron say.

Alison's footsteps backtracked and I tried to feel at ease. I knew that Cade was the one who controlled the visions; whether I was expecting them or not. *Come on Cade, show me. Let me see who it is. Let me catch him.*

No words described the feeling I felt; maybe seasick was close enough. I felt rocky and uneasy repeating the thought he might be here, but then if he wasn't, we would have to start from phase 1 again.

Nothing was happening. I clenched my fists harder, sculpting my fingernails back into my hands. My eyes were closed, but only shapes and colors were leaving them. The twirling spirals and different tones of colors were making me dizzy. It was the same situation when you squeezed your eyes and saw spots when you opened them.

Cade. Show me. Help me. Anything.

My brain started vibrating and triggering a similar feeling. I saw Cade in a small room, dark and rusty. Her body was looking up at a tall figure, his shadow muscular and thick, almost demonic looking from its hunched pose with his hand ready to slap her.

"What is it Cade?" I squeezed my eyes.

"It's not him, he's not there."

"What? I don't get it."

"Look up."

I looked up farther and another vision occurred. It was in the view of Cade's eyes and I saw the man looking down at her. It was the wrong person.

"Two to the left. From the middle. Hurry, Nick."

Her soul disappeared, while a slap in the background sent chills up my spine.

Chapter 14

I opened my eyes and almost fell back. Cameron ran up and caught me, but I fell softly onto the cold marble floor. "What happened?"

"Two from the left. From the middle." I got up and walked over to the bench. I looked away as Alison went into the room to tell the guard.

"What? No! You can't do this."

His cry for help was almost pulling me towards the direction of stopping the scene. But Cade would never lie to me. She would never have the ability to take someone's life away. I knew she was telling the truth, she had to be.

The guards hustled him out of the window and I looked at another suspect dead in the eyes. I showed no mercy, but he was innocent. Still, you had to look or act someway to be in this sort of hell.

"We need to go upstairs."

"No. Stop." I stood up.

"What, Cade?" Ash asked.

"That is not the right guy. I mean- I don't know who he is, but all I know is that he is not the one with Cade right now."

"How do you know?" Alison asked.

"Because I saw a faded look of him. But I can't really remember what he looks like. I just know there is still someone else."

"Is there anything she said?" Alison came over to me.

"I don't remember. But we need to talk to this guy, he obviously has something to do with it."

"I will go talk to him."

"I wanna come." I needed to get answers. Who was this person? Why wasn't he with Cade? There was something connecting the both of them that I simply couldn't put my finger on. The scent of this room was getting to me. It was the smell of criminals. I know there was no distinct smell, but this room sure made it seem like it.

"We need to see who he is, get some answers."

"Where are they taking him now?" Ash asked.

"To a room." Cameron responded, he knew exactly what "room" Alison was talking about.

My body suddenly began to feel unreal. I knew what was going to come of this: torture. It sounded fine, but the true meaning, wouldn't hit me until later. Until there was blood and secrets to be spilled.

"Run a lie detector test." I blurted out.

"What?" Cameron asked.

"Nikki, that's a good idea." Alison called on her radio. "We are gonna do a 49.44 on room 5, suspect 1."

"Ok. Clear." A police officer responded back.

"I want to be in the room."

Alison walked out. She didn't decline my question that came out like a demand. I hope I wasn't being rude because my emotions were catching up to my brain. That doesn't sound right. See? My world was turning me into something that didn't make sense. Nothing made sense to me. Thinking about it, it never did. I never grasped the reason why we we are all here. What our purpose is. By now, you know that I can get off track; don't know why and don't care. It happens and with me, I go with the flow.

We all made our way to Alison's office. I stood near the door making sure no one could hear through.

"Can someone explain to me what is going on?" Ash went over to the chair.

"I told you. That is not the person who is holding Cade right now."

"So what is going?" Cameron asked.

"We are going to run a lie detector test on him. I will let you know what happens, but Nikki, you can come with me."

I had to straighten my shirt and stretch out my leggings. The dust was getting on them and a long strip ran up to my thigh. My hands dusted it off and I combed through my hair. I needed to look serious and intimidating, not that a criminal would find me anyway.

A little puny teenager with her messy brown hair and old shirt and leggings, nothing seems more intimidating than that for sure.

"Boys, stay here. When you are hungry go get something to eat, Rual will watch you." Rual was waiting outside. He reminded me of Dmitry; his tall frame and his stiff posture. Only kind words and connection would turn that straight face into a smile. It took a lot to crack Dmitry, and I finally did. But I was stupid and left our whole relationship when I escaped. What does "relationship" even mean? Children and bodyguards were not supposed to have a relationship, but obviously I couldn't help that we connected.

"Wait." I caught up with Alison and we stopped a few feet

outside her office. "Can you see if you can get ahold of Dmitry from the hospital?"

"Why?"

I looked at my dirty converse. The laces were messed up and tied incorrectly. "Because, I just left him."

"Honey, don't be so hard on yourself."

"Can you still see if he has his job or get his information?"

"I will see what I can do, but right now we need to get this going."

Alison pushed me forward to follow her and we went up stairs.

The lie detector was loud, well, to me anyway. In fact, it was deafening. Picking up a case of stutter or a slight shift in response meant anything in these types of situations. Maybe he was guilty, maybe he was a cheat; there was no way of knowing for sure.

His hands were cuffed behind his back. He softly pulled to loosen the tight grip that made marks on his body. The color of his skin was turning purple on the wrist of his hands. The indent was visible from the entry and I trembled at the sight of it.

Although it hurt to think this man was in pain, I knew he committed a crime. Whether in this situation or another. There was only time that would catch up to him. I didn't get why criminals did what they did. Their purpose behind their masterful plan, it didn't make sense. Maybe they were sad, unhappy, raised poorly. That makes sense, but to possess the will to take someone's life, it sounds insane. No, it sounds inhumane. They are not human. What does it mean to be human? I don't know. Definitely not taking someone's life or ruining it.

I get that people can become depressed and have their own issues, but still. There are ways to solve them but by no means is a solution a killing spree.

I walked in with Alison and clenched my fist, not because I was nervous or mad, but it was a distraction. A way to move through the impulsive decisions or choices I usually made. The criminal's eyes lowered, so I assumed he knew my position. His blank expression suddenly gained a smirk on the top right corner. He lay his head down and watched as the other police officers put the cords around his head and heart.

"I will ask the questions, if you want to ask anything, ask me first. What we say in this room stays in this room." We walked over to the chairs. "We will begin." Alison pressed on the switch and turned the monitoring system on.

"First question, what is your name?"

He didn't move nor say anything. The beeping noise was faint in the background continuing with the same pattern. Up and down and up and down. There was no end to this madness. Every corner there was a surprise. Opening a point of life for me, and everyone else.

"Josh Green." His words spoke. That was a simple name, no criminal connotation or vibe from the pronunciation.

"I have something to ask." I stood up.

"Uh-" Alison was going to stop me, but I moved a little closer to Josh.

"Is that your real name?"

"Yes-yes it is."

The monitor was changing, recording the details of his answers and heartbeat. We would soon find out later if he was telling the truth, but I continued.

"Are you one of the names on the list?"

"What list?"

The monitor stopped and entered a high pitch nose for a quick second.

"What is your name on the list?" I altered my question because I knew I was right.

"Ryan Lib." His eyes lowered. I got him.

"Do you know Cade?"

"Who is that?" He chuckled. "A boy?"

"Do you know Cade?" I stepped on a cord that connected to his arm. It injected some sort of pain into him whenever he wouldn't answer.

"Why would I want a boy? Especially when I can get you?"

My heart stopped. Ew. Gross.

Alison stood up and pressed the pain into him more. Ryan groaned and growled under his breath. It reminded me of those supernatural tv shows. When the bad guy is in the chair tied up, either a vampire or werewolf, growling as its way to protect themselves. However, there was no use in this environment. We could use anything against him, and we would if it meant getting answers.

"Do you know who Cade is?!" I yelled louder and slapped him in the face. After the an imprint was made of his face, I suddenly realized what I had done. I was a hypocrite for beating someone at my will. I had a good reason, but that still didn't make me innocent.

"Nikki." Alison grabbed my arm, but I pulled to let go.

"Yes. I do." He finally let out.

"Are you user504?"

Ryan looked broken and defeated. Good. I'm glad he is.

He deserves whatever shit comes his way.

"The girl asked you a question." Alison rose her voice.

"No. I promise."

Time was up. Alison switched off the monitor and took the cords from his head.

"You know this is a lie detector test, right?" I laughed right in his face.

It was obvious we weren't going to get anything else out of him. If he had any information on Cade, he wasn't going to share. But maybe he was good at lying, or just wanted to save his own skin. But how foolish of him. The whole point of this test was to get around the lies and cheats. We were going to do exactly that.

One of the guards came in and took Ryan from his captive seat. The chains were unlocked but once again his hands were behind his back, tightly. I waited until he was out of the room to ask Alison about the test.

"So, what does it say?"

Alison grabbed the records from the detector. I walked over to her and pressed my fingers into the writing.

"It needs to be about 30 minutes. Let the other officers look over it and make sure everything is right."

"Hey guys." I opened the door to Alison's office. Cameron and Ash were on their phones finishing up a sandwich. I could really use one of those.

"What happened?" Cameron asked.

"We need to wait for the results, but I think we got him." I smiled at Cameron and looked at Ash who stood up to throw away a wrapper.

"Where is Rual?"

"Why?" Ash asked.

"Cause, I'm kind of hungry." I felt my stomach and my dry mouth.

"Then, let's go get something." Cameron opened the door and located his mother.

"Mom." He tilted his head into the hallway. "Have you seen my mom?" Cameron asked one police officer.

"Yes, she went out front."

Cameron looked at me. "Whatever, let's go get Rual, he can take us."

Ash, Cameron and I walked to the front of the building to the desk. "Have you seen Rual?" Ash asked the woman.

"Yes, do you need him?"

"We need to go get something to eat for Nikki." Ash responded.

The woman called for Rual on her radio. I lay my back on the door looking outside the window. Everything was moving fast on the street; the cars, lights and birds. My life was moving slow. Each moment that passed could mean another minute slipping away that we could find Cade. If you really think about it, I'm going to get food right now. I really should be finding Cade and speeding things up.

"Hello. You need to eat?" Rual came up to me.

"Yes."

He opened the door and walked to a black suburban. The license plate was unrecognizable so I'm guessing it was a rental. Figuring Cameron or Ash would sit in the passenger seat in the front, I hopped into the back. I crossed my legs, correcting my posture just to slouch when I put my head on my hand.

"Where do you want to go?" Rual asked.

Junk food was never really something I enjoyed. It always made me feel like crap after, and then I would cry on the phone to Cade explaining how fat I was. However, from all that has been happening to me I craved a chocolate shake.

We stopped at McDonald's and waited in the 20 minute line. Cameron asked if it was really worth staying there for so long, but I told him he was overreacting. My eyes would shut every 30 seconds from exhaustion.

That is one serious problem today, sleep deprivation. I always complained to my teachers something needed to change. They agreed with me in some ways, but I knew they couldn't change anything. When I find Cade that is what we are going to do, write a report about changing the school hours to fit teenagers sleep patterns. Because if you haven't noticed, we are important too.

We finally were up in line. I looked up to the menu scanning all the delicious foods. There was bacon, egg and cheese, ham, honey and mustard. My brain flashed back to a point where Cade and I were so hungry after school that we had our cheat day.

Cheat days were a time that we planned. Once a month, after skipping all the junk food in our houses, we would hit the mall food court. We felt so sick after, but glad we finally waited all this time to eat the ice cream and sundaes. It felt wrong that I made today my cheat day without Cade. I wonder if she knew I was having one. I wonder if Cade's getting food at all; is she starving?

Chapter 15

"What would you like?" asked the McDonald's worker. That scary thought soon faded when I was reminded of the sandwich I was going to order.

"Uh, bacon, egg and cheese please." I smiled and looked at Cameron for reassurance. Cameron knew about our cheat days, so I didn't know if his opinion would change. We came up with strict rules about what we were allowed to eat outside those days. He knew everything, so when he nodded I felt okay about what I was doing.

I waited in the car while Rual and the boys got the order. Something about not drawing attention to myself was what they told me hiding was for. It didn't bother me they were trying to protect me from all the publicity I was getting. There were so many questions to why I ran away and my absence from school. People weren't believing the story that Alison made up for me.

By the time my stomach started growling, the three of them came back to the car. The smell of bacon made my mouth water. My mom was never big on bacon, but I always had to have some. There were times when people just craved things and I needed this.

"Here." Ash handed me the wrapped sandwich.

"Thank you." I ripped open the paper and threw it on the car rug. "I'll pick that up later." My teeth sank into the perfectly heated bacon, egg and cheese. It probably looked like I hadn't eaten in ages.

"We should go back." Cameron jumped into the front car seat. "My mom called. They must be done." Rual slipped into the driver's seat.

My plan was to take my time eating it. So every piece that went into my mouth, I could really taste. Plus, it was healthy in a way so I wasn't having all carbs. Eggs were good for you, and that was always my breakfast. By now you would think I'd be sick of it, but nah. Not really.

The sandwich was digesting into my system. I had burped a few times in the car ride to myself and walking through the hallway to Alison's office. Suddenly, a burst of heat started to take hold of me. Like fire just broke out. I turned around to see Ash walking behind me. "Are you okay?" He came closer and touched my cheek.

Looking both ways, I was sure something touched me. My body was burning and itching; my fingers vigorously scratching my right hand.

"Cameron, you need to see this." Ash said.

I didn't look up at Ash's facial expression, but I knew he thought it was bad. I mean, I was seeing it myself. There were reddish spots on my right hand and my body felt overheated. Cameron ran over and touched me on the back. "Nick, what's wrong?"

I couldn't speak. No words could form to express the confusion and pain I felt. "I-I."

"What, Nick?!" Cameron asked. The only thing I was sure of right now was Cameron's concern for me. His eeriness touched my skin. Almost making the pain go away, just a little. I felt like a marshmallow being toasted, but too hard. Becoming burnt with no taste anymore.

"Sit down." I managed to say. There was a seat a few feet away from me. My hands were wrapped around Cameron and Ash, as they were walking me to the bench. "Take off." I motioned to my sweatshirt on top of me. Ash zipped it open and Cameron ran to get me water. My vision was perfectly clear so this was not another vision; and I don't think a sandwich could do this to me. It felt more personal.

"Drink."

Cameron handed me the cup. The water ran through my veins and provided some way for the heat to escape. But after that, it went right back to steaming hot.

"Somebody get Alison!" Rual finally spoke. I forgot he was there, watching the whole thing. Maybe he was thinking I was faking this, so people could feel bad for everything that I went through. Probably because he didn't feel bad for me. But everyone has their own opinions and I guess losing a best friend doesn't shock him as sad or believable.

"Can you hear me, Nick?" Cameron felt my head. "She's burning up." He cupped my arm and tried to block me from itching the spots.

I took a deep breathe. Like someone just put my voice back into my body. "What is happening?!" Then I started crying. I didn't even realize I was until Ash was on the other side of me wiping the tears from my face.

"You are burning up." Cameron told me.

Alison finally made her way over to me. She was running with a first aid kid. I'm sure nothing in there could help.

"What happened, Cameron?"

"I don't know, she just started burning up, look at her arms."

Alison rolled over both my arms. I was still crying.

"Could this have anything to do with Cade?"

Alison looked at Cameron, who looked at Ash. They couldn't answer because they didn't know. Neither did I.

"I'm calling the Ambulance."

"Ah." A shrieking voice started in my head. I was becoming dizzy and losing vision. I ran over to the closest garbage can and vomited.

"What is it, Nikki?" Ash rubbed my back.

"Nikki- help. It's so hot. I- I can't."

I turned around to Cameron and Ash. "It's Cade."

"What is she saying, where is she?"

"I can't see her." I started to blink fast looking at both of them.

"Close your eyes, Nick."

So I closed my eyes, but there was nothing.

"Why isn't it working?" Ash asked.

Finally my eyes shut, not my control, but Cade's. She forced them together and provided a clear image. Gruesome as I might add. Cade was lying on the ground with fire right next to her. The man was a shadow that took the torch burning her and smearing the ashes around the edges of her body.

'Ahh." I touched my leg while the man touched Cade's. He kicked her. He kicked me. He kicked us.

"Nick!" Cameron held onto me from falling. I wonder where Ash was. Maybe Cameron jumped in before.

Then another sharp pain stabbed me in the bottom of my foot. It almost felt as if someone was engraving a message. A call for help. From who? Cade? The man? I had to look- it was so painful.

"What is that?" Cameron asked.

O-M-G. He sees it. Wait? He sees it? This hasn't happened before.

"Nick, I see it."

"What is it?"

"How can I see it?" Cameron asked.

"I don't know." I responded.

Then Ash was there. "See what?" He added.

"Help, Cameron."

He pulled me into his chest. "Hold on. Breathe." He whispered.

"Nick. I love you." Cade looked at me. Her eyes piercing. They were filled with fire. Like she was born from the devil.

"I love you too, Cade." That was it. My eyes opened. Those three words meant everything, but they would mean more if we could actually find her.

Chapter 16

"Are you okay?"Cameron asked as I was walking back to the chair.

"Yeah, that was scary. Why can't Ash see it?" I turned to him.

"I don't know. Maybe Cade wanted me to?" He sounded shocked.

"This is too much. I can't."

"Stop, Nikki. You can."

"Please- forget about it for now."

"It might be important, Nikki."

"Please." I begged.

"Alright."

"So, Cade was torturing you?" Alison asked, her arms crossed.

"It wasn't like that."

"Then what is it like?" Alison countered back. I know she wasn't trying to sound rude or make me feel like Cade was the villain, but it did come off the wrong way. Yes it was true, Cade was somehow showing me her pain. But I think it was more meant as a connection, so we'd struggle together. The pain hurt like hell, when doesn't pain hurt? But I get what Alison was trying to say. I just hope she didn't truly believe it herself. I wondered if I was making a mistake by hiding the mark.

I ignored the question and tried to focus towards something else. "Did you look at the report?"

"Yes, I did."

"And?"

Cameron and Ash came a little bit closer.

She smiled. "He is lying. He knows Cade."

"I knew it." My mind was racing. His useless and old smell and posture. Scary, but sure. Mentally stable was the way to pronounce what was happening. It almost didn't seem possible for him to understand the consequences he would get. Hell didn't even understand. Well- actually I'm sure hell did. I was ready for him to face eternity struggling for air in the downworld. Soon his leader would be with him, both struggling. But until then, may he crash and burn for all I care.

Chapter 17

"Before we do anything, you need to see your parents. Talk to them or something." Alison's voice was loud.

I rolled my eyes and turned back to her. She was right. It's been a few weeks since I really sat and had a deep conversation with them. "Ok, who's gonna take me?"

"Rual. They are waiting for you at my house. You can still stay with me. We'll come here tomorrow and start getting more answers."

I sighed. Whether it was from depression or relief, I couldn't tell. But it was clear enough that I did feel a certain way, there was just no way to tell which I was feeling.

Cameron and Ash stayed behind. I told them I needed to talk to my parents alone. Of course I wanted them there, I just thought It would be more respectful. Except I was hoping for time to move fast. There was no point to drag on about my last few experiences because they wouldn't believe me. My own parents. Born from the same blood and veins- somehow wouldn't believe me. I couldn't take that chance.

Well that was something. I walked up to the guest room I've been sleeping in with Cameron and Ash. The talk between me, my mom and dad just finished and I didn't know what we really talked about. It was along the lines of, "I'm sorry for escaping, there is just stuff I can't explain right now, but trust me Alison is taking care of me." They accepted what I said and surprisingly, didn't disagree. They told me all that mattered was my safety. I knew they were confused in the phrase "I can't explain right now." However, they trusted Alison and knew her judgement was professional. I said I would call them everyday or shoot them a text, but judging how far I've gotten finding Cade that part might be a little doubtful.

The talk was about an hour. They brought me more clothes and proper toiletries that Cameron or Ash somehow couldn't get. My computer was a vital object I was missing. Whenever I need to destress, I would go on buzzfeed and take random quizzes. It was insanely creepy how accurate they were, but they helped me calm down.

Climbing into bed, I unfolded my favorite pink blanket. I opened my laptop and directly headed for the buzzfeed website. The quizzes lined up on the left sides with their bolded headings. I scanned through them looking for one I wanted to take. The ones about personalities were my favorite; they would either tell me I was a rebel or cunning so I always expected to get something like that.

I clicked on the one that said build your ice cream and we will tell you something about yourself. The first question was pick a flavor: Chocolate. The second question was pick a topping: Sprinkles. The third question was another topping: strawberries. The fourth question was cone or cup: Cone. The final question was whipped cream, fudge or nothing: Nothing.

Ambitious but lonely

Ambitious I could live with. But lonely? Did my ice cream flavors really feel reveal that? I struggled with the response for a second. To admit to something like was admitting to vulnerability. I hate being vulnerable.

In order to see if they were accurate I plugged in all my friends. I did Cameron first.

Vanilla, oreo bits, blueberries, cup and fudge. Charming but secretive

This was hard. Did I find Cameron secretive? Could this be a sign he felt something for me? My tutor always told me he didn't believe in signs, they were just somehow coincidental.

Then I did Ash.

Mint Chocolate chip, gummy bears, raspberries, cone, nothing. Tough but shy

Now this was true. From the moment I met Ash, he couldn't quite get his feelings out there, but once did, his real personality kicked in.

I thought about putting in Cade's choices.

Vanilla, sprinkles, mango, cup and whipped cream.

Vibrant but isolated.

If you think my reaction was quick, don't. I didn't want to treat Cade like she wasn't alive. I was being hopeful, first time in ages.

The word isolated made me feel sick. They all were accurate, which made me believe I was lonely. I am surrounded by people who care about me, but why am I still lonely with these people?

What I wanted from these quizzes was relief and easiness, but all they did was just spike my emotions. They popped a bubble that was peacefully floating and made me angry.

Why is no one enough? Or, Is it that i'm not enough for them? I shut my computer a little too hard and knocked it off my bed, digging my head into my pillow.

Damn you buzzfeed.

Chapter 18

My mom always told me it was normal for girls to feel like this. What would you describe *this* feeling exactly? Jealousy, unworthiness, depression? So many words, for so many people. I can't tell you how much I've wanted to curl up in a ball and hide. That seems like a solution. But is it really?

I happen to think people create scenarios in their mind. They make their own hate and think people are after them. I've gone insane many times, trust me when I say this. For example, when I was at school with Cade I always felt people were looking at us. My mom told me I was overreacting. Another time was when I found a note in my locker from someone, a love note you could say. It turned out to be a guy playing a joke on me. Cameron found out and threw a punch at the dude; he got suspended.

So see? Sometimes I'm not completely losing my mind. If I told my mom how I felt right now, she wouldn't help much. She would say what any mother *should* say: "You're beautiful, inside and out." But we know, as girls, this means nothing to us.

I know I have Ash. We've been together for a while, and don't get me wrong. He is what I want overall, I just felt like there was a deeper connection with Cameron. It had nothing to do with their looks.

The door opened and the curtains drew in the light. It was too early for this. The sun was calling for me to get a move on. It's blinding power was drawing me back to sleep. Heat makes me tired. Whenever I use a heating pad for cramps I always fell asleep.

The boys yawned and got up from their blow-ups. The housekeeper left the room, I was left in bed. My body was under the covers in this warm ball. I wasn't ready to face the world. Somebody could never wake me up and I wouldn't know how much time passed. That was how comfortable I was.

"Nick, get up." Cameron said. Both of the boys came over to my bed. Ash pulled the covers off and I laughed.

"No." I whined and put a pillow over my head.

"My mom says it's important."

I struggled to get up and tried to ignore the pain in my back. The feeling was dull but sharp at the same time. I tried to release the pain with tennis balls as my dad used to tell me. Didn't help much after discovering my spine was uneven; I had to be in a back cast for a month.

"How did the talk with your parents go?" Ash asked while changing his shirt.

"Really?" Cameron asked as we both looked at this naked top.

Ash chuckled. " We're all friends here. Not like we haven't seen anything before."

I coughed while Cameron's face began to blush. Why was he? I assumed him and Cade took it to the next level. Especially since their relationship was so close. Cade would always talk to me about how she trusted him, but never mentioned if they did it or not.

I don't know if Cameron thought Ash and I did it. Cause that would be a no.

"It was good, thanks."

Cameron took off his shirt. I was choosing the clothes I wanted to wear, but seeing Cameron, I stopped. Literally. I put my t-shirt and leggings down and looked for three complete uncomfortable seconds at Cameron's body.

But don't get me wrong, Ash's was quite something too. I hoped he didn't notice the way I looked at Cameron. How my eyes sort of twinkled in a radius only someone who was standing a few inches of me could see. The way my lips folded to make a crescent smirk. I bit my lip and looked down into my bag.

There was pile of clothing, but all I saw was a black hole. One I'd be lost in forever.

Chapter 19

"*Are you ner*vous?" Cameron asked?

We were outside the parking lot in the car. I managed to be in front with Cameron who was driving. I looked at the door wondering what was beyond. When I looked at it, I always felt it was a block. A wall that separated our world from theirs. By that I mean, the criminals. Everything changed for them once they went in. Some made it out alive and had the chance to escape that world, but most, ended up there for good. Thank you for that.

"No I'm fine." And I actually was, I think.

"It's okay to be nervous."

"I know. I know." I wanted to stop his lecture. I wanted this. It was my decision.

"Can we go?" Ash laughed and opened the car door.

I laughed. Always there to break the silence. I was wondering if I'd be there to break his heart.

We all walked next to each other, distancing ourselves to make it seem like we weren't hiding anything. I mean, we weren't hiding anything, but we had a tendency to act like that.

"Where is Alison?" Cameron walked to the front desk.

The women officer pointed down to her office. Cameron took the lead and walked in with a confident attitude. Much more than anything I had these past weeks.

"Hi mom."

Alison looked up from scratching notes on her pad.

"Are we going to see the guy now?"

"About that-." Alison stood up and picked the navy folder beside her scissors.

"What?" I hoped she wasn't going to say I couldn't go. Maybe because I slapped him last time, during the lie detector test? It couldn't be for that silly reason. Not that it was a mistake or anything. It was skin touching skin. Not playful, but certainly not violent enough. I could have used my claws, or nails, towards his face.

"I got the address." She handed me the classified paper, but I only saw the slip on the first page.

I traced my finger onto each word.

"Wait. Why did you do it without me?" I asked.

"Because, I didn't want you to be in there while I was doing it."

"But you knew I wanted to be."

"Nick, she was doing it to protect you."

I chuckled and turned around with the folder. "Well, then. I'm coming with you."

"No, you are not."

"What?!"

"Mom?" Cameron asked shocked.

"This is dangerous, we have a killer on our hands. I have to keep you safe."

"But-."

"No arguments."

"Cameron!" I was getting worried they weren't going to know where to look. I was the only one with the psychic power to reach Cade. If it weren't for me, we would have no lead.

"We need backup for route 3."

What did that mean?

"Nikki. My mom is right."

"What?" I clenched my fist. Ok, now I wanted Ash.

"This isn't fair Alison." Ash stepped in, I relaxed my fingers.

Alison walked out of the room while I stayed behind with the two boys.

"Are you serious, Cameron?"

"Nope." He pulled out his car keys and twirled them around his finger.

"Screw you." I laughed and walked over to punch his shoulder.

"Man, that was good Cameron." Ash commented.

We waited for the police cars to leave the station so no one was suspicious of us following them.

When we were in the clear we walked to the car pretending to talk on the way out. I linked hands with Ash and walked to the car. I was traumatized by the fact we were looking for Cade. How there was a slim chance her body might be broken. Locked under the green grass and shaded sky, unable to walk and talk on this earth again.

"Are you okay?" Cameron asked while we were driving about five minutes away from the address. It's a good thing Alison showed me the address, even though, her intention was not for me to come with her.

"Yea-." I stopped because I heard a loud sound hitting the door. I rolled down the window and rain started hitting the ground. This reminded me of the time I saw Cade, in the car crash. She was drenched looking at me. I closed my eyes and replayed the scene in my head hoping when I opened them I would see Cade. Though, somehow, she would be wearing something more colorful and her hair would be dry. And this dark and cloudy weather would be full of love and life. When I hoped for a dream, I was oblivious to reality. No one was in front of us. Only the sweeping of dust in the car and loud droplets shattering my heart.

I looked at Cameron. "I'm sorry."

"I know." he said.

"Uh, did I missing something?" Ash chimed in.

"Ash." Cameron tapped the steering-wheel.

I saw Ash's face in the mirror, he bit his lip when he came to the realization that the conversation was about the crash.

"Oh, I'm sorry." Ash's head sunk.

"I know. Don't worry." I reached back and rubbed his sneaker for a quick second.

"Are we sure we are doing this?" Cameron asked.

"Just go."

We entered the driveway what looked like an abandoned building. The grounds were covered with rotten gum and debri. The smell was fumed with poison like animals had died here. It was far from the street for anyone to notice a couple of kids were here alone. We made our way into an open parking lot space, handicapped I might add, as it was the farthest from the cars.

There were empty police cars in the driveway; we got out of the car and shut the doors quietly. I could sense a battle coming for me. Dark and light fighting. I know there is a demon inside of us all. I was wondering when my demon side would come out- or if it has already. I would never drop to the level of a killer, but if it meant saving my best friend, then I will become *that* killer.

Chapter 20

"Be quiet." Cameron said while I stepped on the rocks following into the building.

"Sorry." I whispered.

We made our way into the back of the building, past the trees and small bushes. I peeked into the window and saw Alison leading the pack. Ash gave me a little push to move on; I almost tripped. He laughed and his contagious smile caused me to laugh after him. I covered my mouth and told Ash to shut up because we were going to get in trouble.

As we entered the back of the building, I thought I heard a stomping in the house. "Come on." Ash said. Cameron opened the door slightly. The entrance was clean and clear. The house was emptied, but the cracks on the top of the walls gave away the motive. It meant to look like a house, but it could be used for anything. The right person had to find it, and they did. For the wrong reason, of course.

"Where are they?" I stuck by Cameron and Ash.

"Stop." Ash walked in front of us. I heard a gunshot. Cameron's hand smacked onto my lips before I let out a scream. My eyes widened and I felt like I was in a horror movie. This was all pretend. I was dreaming, somebody pinch me. A tear dropped from my eye.

It better not be Cade. Oh god, what if it is? Oh shit, no. Cameron nodded and smiled at me. A comfort smile was his intention, but no one could make me shake the feeling I was going to die, or that Cade died before me.

I grabbed Cameron and Ash's hand, I was pressed between them trying to keep my mouth from speaking. It blew my mind they continued to walk after hearing the gunshot; in movies they would run, but this was no movie.

We creeped into the kitchen area, though, it didn't look much like a kitchen. When we got closer into the building, I heard the footsteps again. I turned to a door, like a basement. It was cracked in half, dots of blood covered the knob. Gulping, I looked at Cameron and Ash. There were holes on the white door and I scraped my finger on the edges. "What if other kids are down there with Cade?"

"Sh, just go." Ash said.

Cameron walked before me as went down the stairs. I heard footsteps walking before us.

"It's my mom." Cameron said looking at the corner. We were on the edge of the stairs peeking our way into the space.

"Keep moving." Alison led the group farther.

"Let's go." Cameron said.

Our steps were silent, trying to keep our toes from touching the wooden floor. The creaks made my heart jump. I was worried people were going to notice we were here.

"Stop." Alison said.

Cameron turned around and put his hand over my mouth. How did he know I was gonna say something? Or that I was thinking about screaming?

The footsteps were getting closer to us. Ash held my hand in the back of my sweatshirt.

"Go. Go." Cameron pushed me a little bit.

We made it up two stairs with Alison stopping us. "What the hell are you guys doing here?!"

"Mom-"

"No. You are leaving. Take them out."

"Alison, we got a signal." Another police officer said.

"I want to come." I added.

"You could get hurt, this is no place for children."

"I will guard them." An officer stepped forward. It was illegal for us to be here, and that's how it should be. There's no way children were meant for this environment. Even adults. I focused on the possibility of dying. Being obliterated into thin air, by fire or having us gutted by knives until we bleed. There were so many ways to die. Haven't you ever heard of 1,000 dumb ways to die? This would be one of them. Off my bucket list.

"This is absurd."

"Guys, we need to go." Another officer said.

"Stay behind, and be quiet."

We stepped down the stairs with two guards in front of us. I heard the beeping sound in the front of the guards, with Alison pointing her gun out. It didn't seem so realistic. I was hunting down a bad guy, trying to find my best friend.

"What was that?" I heard footsteps as the noise beeped louder.

"Who's there?" Another voice said.

"Sh, Nikki, be quiet!" Alison stammered.

The door opened and out came a man holding a gun. He pulled the trigger and shot one of the guards. It wasn't Alison, but I buried my face into Cameron's shoulder. The guards took us to the left side to hide behind a wall.

Bullets are for the weak, scars are for the brave. A knife has the power to kill a life, its soul purpose is to cut. Food, hands, skin. All of the above.Taking my fist I want to shatter this wall. It's looking at me like I'm stupid. What's a couple of bricks got on me? Well, It's keeping me from climbing and falling hard.

"Mom!" Cameron yelled.

"Stay back, kid."

I looked at Cameron; this was all my fault.

I am the source of destruction and I hurt everyone.

Chapter 21

Getting myself into this mess wasn't a choice. It was an obligation. Whatever you or the world considers a mess; I was pretty sure this was one. But my philosophy is this: I'd have to go in, in order to get out. That doesn't really make sense, but I promise you in the end it will- hopefully.

"Need backup, man down." Alison's voice was distant, but loud enough. Cameron sighed and I was relieved.

"Stay behind me."

We walked into the room. You would not believe what I saw next. Alison came over before I could scan the whole room. "Take them out."

I moved her hand out of the way. "Stop." Walking forward, a vomit taste in my mouth started to touch the tip of my tongue. A man was shot to death on the right side of the floor. The blood was seeping through his chest. I looked away trying to tell myself he was dead. Where did his soul go? It better be in hell.

Boys were passed out on the ground, between the age of five to twelve. Police officers walked to the ones who were still breathing. How did anyone have the heart to do this? My heart was becoming non-existent, slipping away. Wanting to crumble. I called out for Cade.

"Cade?" I walked around the room, ignoring the children. I started to cry, there was no sign of her. The string was still attached, but no visions would help me at this point. Backup was called through the radio. I called for Cade again. Her name left an imprint in the room. Her soul was a ghost lost in sight. No one could find her.

Within seven minutes, more followed in as we rounded up the bodies we saw. It was time consuming-or that's just my excuse to take away the pain of seeing these bodies. One of them could have been Cade. I can't think like that. God was helping me find her and I was thankful for that. But man, was I mad at God. How evil could God be to take my best friend? Make us all lose our minds and think we were supposed to cope? Did god truly think that? It's astonishing how much power God can give and take away within seconds, moments of a life. Moments of my life. I swear if we don't find Cade, God will have to pay.

"Where is Cade?" I ran over to Alison.

"I don't know. He gave me this address."

"You mean, you don't know if Cade was going to be here?" That was it; I was losing my mind. I was losing my purpose. I was losing my best friend. A shatter in my heart broke the hope I had. There was a slight chance Cade was going to be in one piece looking at me like I had saved her. That was a dream. It wouldn't matter how much I wanted it to exist because it wouldn't, and it never would.

"We need to go now." Alison touched my shoulder.

"I'm not going with you." I ran away from the scene to the car outside.

Cameron and Ash followed me. I didn't make it very far falling on the grass outside. The muddy ground stained my shirt, but I didn't move. Softly, the wind was blowing on me, making me feel a little calmer. I wished for a world where I was happy. That's what shooting stars were for- and I haven't seen one in ages. Maybe that was my problem. I needed a shooting star. *You are crazy, Nikki. This is insane.*

I started to cry and put my ear to the grass. I felt Cade's breath, and I heard her. I saw a shadow in front of me on the road. "Cade." I gasped. Her leggings were torn and her shirt was ripped from the sides.

"You aren't going to make it, Nikki."

"Stop, Cade. Stop." I got up walking closer to her.

"Nikki." Cameron was running in background.

"Nikki, it's okay."

"Stop, Cade." I put my hand on her cheek not knowing I could actually touch her. I looked at my hand, then back at Cade whose eyes were in shock too.

"How is this happening, Cade?"

"I- I don't know."

"I mean, everything. Not just this."

"I don't know."

"Where are you?"

"He's coming. Hurry up. Talk to the boy."

"Which boy?" There was so many boys.

"You will know."

"Cade!" my hand was now touching air.

"Nick, are you okay?"

"We aren't going to make it in time." I was too tired to cry, too tired to talk. The ground seemed like a good place to land. I thought I might take a nap; I gave up and fell into Cameron's arms. His sweet cologne was comforting.

"Nikki." A voice in the background woke me up.

"She is sleep deprived." Ash's voice said.

"She's upset."

"Guys." I stood up and yawned. The soft couch made my butt feel warmer than usual. My shirt still stained with the brown mud from falling and my leg started to tingle. "Ugh, my foot." Standing up from the bed, I stomped my foot on the ground until the sparks went away.

"Are you okay?" Cameron asked.

"Yeah." I felt my head.

"You should eat something."

Then I remembered what Cade said. There was no time; I needed to get to the boy like Cade said before…. Before, you know what. I don't want to say it, and you are not going to make me.

"We need to go." I walked and stumbled, but Ash caught me before I hit the floor.

"Go where?" Cameron asked.

"To- to the hospital."

"Why?"

"I need to see a boy." I let go of Ash's arms and walked out of the door hoping the boys would follow me.

"What boy?" Cameron got the keys and followed me into the car.

I kept repeating what Cade told me. *You aren't going to make it, you aren't going to make it*. Right now, I needed to be optimistic. I needed to be my own superhero and save myself before I saved Cade. If I didn't believe in me then there was no point, it was half the hope to finding Cade.

I got in the back because I knew Ash would want to sit in the front.

"Why are you going back there?" Cameron asked.

"What do you mean?"

"Nevermind." Cameron sounded hurt, and confused.

"How do you know which boy?"

I didn't answer Cameron because I didn't know. It seemed pointless wasting my breath on the unknown. No one had heard it besides me, because no one could see Cade or hear her. For the first time I felt stupid, like possibly God was against me. I always felt some sort of distance between me and my own life. That didn't make sense- I know. But think about it like this, your life is a person and it is battling you. Yet, at the same time it gives you these rewards and memories, then can change whenever. That was my life, a person, trying to bring me down and lift me up at the randomest moments of times.

Cameron's phone started to ring. "Hey, mom."

I couldn't hear the other line. "What is she saying?"

"We are going to the hospital."

He stopped.

"No- you don't." He hung up the phone.

"What happened?" I asked.

"She wants to come to the hospital."

"But-."

'What's wrong with that?" Ash didn't get it. Nothing was really *wrong* with Alison coming- I just hoped she wouldn't get in the way of anything. I was trying to find this boy that Cade was talking about and the last thing I wanted or needed were distractions.

The word distractions had many meanings in my life right now. One of those meanings was this love triangle, that I admit I'm in. Two boys, two looks and two different meanings in my life. What exactly are those meanings you might ask?

Cameron: The hero, the charming, the brother, the best friend, the maybe I was in love with him whole time thing

Ash: My bad boy, strong, sensitive, romantic, caring, my partner in crime

Does that answer your question? It's enough admitting this is rattling my brain- but Cade didn't know and there was no way to tell her.

"Nothing, I just didn't want a lot of company." I looked at Cameron who silently chuckled with a knowing look.

"We're here." Ash said. My head was resting on my right hand against the window. I knew this position was going to leave my wrist feeling like it had played three straight games of softball in a row.

We walked inside the hospital entering the counter. "We are here to see the boys involved-"

"Yes, you must be Cameron. Your mom called."

"Oh, Okay. Thank you."

"This way."

We followed the nurse up the stairs to facilities spread out across the floor. How would we know which one Cade spoke of?

"Your mom will be here soon."

I waited for the nurse to leave so I could panic. "What are we going to do?"

"What do you mean?"

"There are so many kids, like 10, how am I supposed to know which one?" I responded.

"You will know- like you always have." Ash came up to me and touched me on the shoulder.

"Thanks." I gave a small smile, hiding my teeth.

"Let's start in the first room."

We walked to the room on the right side. Ash led instead of Cameron and opened the blue curtains. The smell of the hospital was hard to forget. I remembered it since I hurt myself. I was stuck here for hours while the doctors looked at my back; they finally diagnosed it and here I am today happy and healthy. Well- let's re-check that. Not happy or healthy. Just sad and depressed you could say.

"Hi- we are hear to speak with him." Cameron said gently to the nurse who was checking the water injected into his body.

"Okay, I will be back." The nurse left the room and closed the curtains. The vibe felt the same and nothing led me to believe this was the boy who I was supposed to see.

"How are you feeling?" Ash said walking up to him. All I could do was look at the way he slurped his tea. He wanted to get it over with. He knew it was healthy for him and would help him get better, but deep down it was like this poison. He wanted to suffer the pain as quickly as possible, like a bandaid being ripped off.

"Anything you want to say?" Cameron asked me.

"Why are you drinking the tea so weirdly?"

The boy looked up at me. His eyes widened and he put the white glass mug down on the tray in front of him.

"Who are you?"

"Who are you?" I went closer to him. Something pulled me to him like a magnet.

"I'm-I'm…. I don't know you."

"We don't bite." Ash chuckled.

"I'm Nikki."

He dropped the eye contact and his shoulders shrugged. His tea almost spilled onto his ugly uniform.

"You." He pointed.

"What?"

"I know you." He said softly.

Chapter 22

"Him." A voice whispered into my ear.

I turned around to the boys. "Did you hear that?"

"Hear what?" Cameron asked.

"Him." It was clear. Cade's voice was telling me I was right. My intuition led us to the right room.

"How do you know me?"

He looked down at this palm; two scars almost parallel to each other.

"You can talk to us." Cameron put his hand over the kid's shoulder.

"What is your name, Kid?" Ash asked.

"It's- Timothy." He looked up to us with uncertain eyes.

"Well, Hi Timothy. Is it possible to know how you know me?" I pulled up a chair and sat a few inches from him. Wanting to give Timothy his space, my motive was to get my point across and find out why he was so important.

Timothy was not speaking anymore. Maybe he needed Allison to make him feel safe. "Call your mom."

"Why?" Cameron asked.

"Ask her how far she is, he needs to feel safe."

Cameron hesitantly took out his phone.

We waited about a minute to hear Alison on the other line.

"Mom- where are you?"

"We are fine. Just need you. You said you were coming."

He hung up his phone. "She will be here soon."

It finally hit me, the way death hits you. I realized I was living in a bubble, protected from what really goes on out there. My mother always told me about the stories on the news, but it never occurred to me it could happen. Especially to someone like Cade.

Alison finally came and sat on the side trying to express her sympathy for this ten year old boy. His eye was badly beaten and his body looked puny; a raisin that grew older and riper, but I was too busy to realize the physical shape he was in. Timothy was wrapped comfortably in a blue blanket the hospital provided.

"Hi, honey." Alison touched the boy's arm. Timothy was shy the way he looked at her.

He kept his hands locked together, stuck like that was his weapon. Silence. It was one. I knew.

"Honey, we need to know more about what happened and how you were abused."

The boy's head stuck to the ground. His eyes wandering somewhere else.

Enough of being nice and trying to ease the words out of this boy's mouth. He said he knew me and that was confusing.

"Do you know Cade?" My tone was harder.

"Yes." His whiny voice barely audible. My eyes lifted, I had got somewhere.

"Where is she? Do you know?" I felt like my voice was attacking him. My grip hard knuckling the cotton blankets.

"I was with her." He coughed. "For a few days."

"And what happened?" My head moved towards him.

"He took her."

"Who?"

"Him."

"Who!" God dammit.

"Him." His hands held on tighter to the blue blanket. I changed my answer. "Why?"

He bit his blanky. "She is the only girl."

Chapter 23

I looked at Alison, with disbelief. My first thought was rape. But somehow I had known it was happening already. He was *raping* her. Then he must of been raping them all. This was not right, this was gross. Oh god, oh god. This was not possible. The only girl, suffering the most, who was still in the hands of the boss. Whatever his name was, it didn't matter. He was alone with her. In a room, quiet and dark. Cade's scream would not be heard within miles, feet, inches, without getting abused. Her only hope for survival was me.

"This is not happening." I said under my breathe.

"Do you know the name?" Alison asked.

Alison's phone started to ring. "Hello?" I looked at Cameron and Ash. "I told you to get the address." Her voice was becoming angry; almost panicked. "How can that be?" Her voice in shock. "Alright, thank you for calling." She hung up the phone.

"What was it, mom?"

'The henchmen, he's dead."

"How? Why?"

"He got murdered, it was an inside job. I don't know how."

"What are we going to do now?" I asked.

"Nothing, we do nothing."

"Huh?" Ash asked.

"Just wait."

"Do you remember anything else?" Alison turned to the boy.

"He drew on me."

"What do you mean?" I asked.

He pointed to the bottom of his foot; Alison and I walked to the left one. We looked at the sole of his foot. A type of bone was drawn; black and white.

"What is that?" Cameron came over asking.

I started to become dizzy remembering the pain I was feeling in the police office. The heat and adrenaline running through my body.

"Are you okay, Nick?" Ash asked.

This was not possible. I hope this was a bad guess and it wouldn't be right. I walked over to the chair and took of my sock and shoe.

"Cameron." I said calling for him.

"What are you doing?" Alison asked.

"You don't think-."

I stopped Cameron.

There it was. A wishbone, the exact one the boy had in the exact same place.

"God." I gasped.

Cameron's eyes widened. He shook his head steadily, resisting the truth.

Alison walked over.

A tear dropped from Cameron's eye.

Why was he crying?

I'm the one with the mark.

Alison connected the two. "That means Cade has one. Wait."

Alison took of her shoe and sock. *No, no. Do not be what I think it is. Stop, Alison. Stop, Alison. Stop God, stop hurting us.*

She popped her eyes up at me. "Mom?" Cameron asked.

She started to cry. "I might know who did this." Ash and Cameron walked over to Alison and me, looking at the bottom of our feet.

"Mom- no, this can't be."

"I'm sorry, Cam. I didn't want to tell you."

"How did you know?"

"The day when Cade told us about the DNA, she mentioned something happening to your mom." Though, Cade was a little off when she said Alison was the one who cheated.

I was shaken by the fact this man also took Alison. When? Why? How? It was probably for a night or so since we didn't notice her absence before.

"But, mom?" Cameron started to cry and the pain was clear. Clear as day and cold as night. I was cold and goosebumps formed on my arms. Alison walked over to Cameron to grab him by the shoulders; he resisted and I never felt more broken in my life.

"Who is it?' I finally managed to say. I wiped the tears from my eyes.

"We are going, now." said Alison.

I put my shoe back on.

"We are going to see him. Come, right now."

I put my sock back on running to catch up with the rest of them.

"When I was hurting in the police office. It was the drawing. I saw some sort of V, but I know now. Cade was being tattooed and so was I."

"It makes sense." Cameron said. "Mom- I'm sorry."

"I know, honey. I know you are."

"What does that mean though?" Cameron asked. He was playing dumb, he knew what it meant, but he didn't want to admit it to himself. Cameron was too wrapped up in the idea of his mom being taken and raped. He couldn't wrap his head around it.

"I don't remember everything honey, I try not to think about it."

"Then how did you know who it is?"

"I'm not sure, but there was only one person who knew what happened to me. But I never believed it."

"So we are we going?"

"Meet me at 54 Bridge Port. I'm going to bring backup."

At least we had a plan. No it wasn't a plan. It was a step. In order for us to have a plan we would need about 10 more steps. In order to find Cade we would need a miracle. Nothing felt like a miracle.

The ride was nothing but voices screaming inside my head. A matter a fact, there was a choice I needed to make. This love triangle needed to end; that meant hearts would be broken or I would end up breaking myself. But nothing would be worse than experiencing the pull between two forces; light and dark, south and east, chocolate or vanilla. You get the point.

I looked at Cameron who was in the front, driving. His head was lost in the road, his mind wandering somewhere else. Behind, Ash was fidgeting with his hands, overwhelmed by being caught in the middle of something like this. He was in pain, and my choice would hurt him more. Yes, you probably know who I chose now, but I don't want to feel guilty about this choice. We were going to find Cade, and that meant, no Cameron.

Cameron: My night and shining armor. I didn't expect how to tell Cameron I wanted to be with him. Who knows if he even felt the same way. We did share a kiss, but that was a while ago.

"Guys. I need to talk to you." I said blankly. Awkwardly, I started the conversation hoping I wouldn't be too weird about it.

"Ok, about what?"

"This isn't the place I wanted to do it, but it needs to be said."

"Ok. And?" Cameron asked.

"So- Cameron and I kissed." *Ouch.*

"What?" When?" Ash shot back.

"A while ago- before we started talking again."

"I can't believe you. When were you gonna tell me?"

"Dude, I'm sorry. Give her a break- it's my fault."

"I'm sorry- I didn't mean to hurt you." I said.

"No, I get it. You're right." Ash said.

"What do you mean?"

"*You* guys."

What did he mean?

"What about us?" Cameron asked.

"You love her." Ash said softly. His words speaking truth and honesty.

I could almost hear a small gulp in Cameron. His cheeks reddening in the mirror.

"And you love him." Ash turned around; not angry, but wise.

"Is that true?" Cameron stopped the silence.

"Do you love me?" I asked.

"You know I do, Nikki."

"Are you in love with her?" Ash asked.

"Uh-yes." He said.

My heart was a song. Beating fast.

"So am I."

Cameron looked up in the mirror and smiled. Our eyes sharing a long enough moment to know we were on the same page.

"I'm okay, Nick. Close friends it is." Ash said.

"I would like that." I smiled.

We stopped at a nice looking suburban house; a yellow door and grey exterior. Alison got out in front of us with police cars driving in. "Where are we?" I looked to Alison who came in the middle of us.

Then the realization hit him. "Mom- It can't be."

Chapter 24

"Who is it?" I asked.

"No, mom."

"I think so." A tear from Alison's eyes dropped. "Let's go." We followed Alison up the curb into the house.

An officer went before us knocking on the door beside Alison.

"Yes?" A kind women opened the door. "Is everything okay?" She asked confused. I was confused as well. I seemed to be the only one who couldn't put the pieces together.

"We are the police."

"Come in." She opened the door a little bit wider. A small boy was standing in the background near a table of pictures.

"How may I help you?" She asked.

"Is your husband home?" Alison asked.

"No- I thought he went to work."

"Your husband doesn't work on Mondays." Another officer said.

"He told me he was going to help out today, with the investigation of a girl..... Cade?"

A tear dropped from my eye hearing that name.

"Mam, don't be alarmed, but I am going to need pictures of your family together."

"Why?" She asked.

"Daddy doesn't like taking pictures." The little boy interrupted.

"How come?"

"He just doesn't." The mother saved the child from almost saying something wrong.

"I need to see a photo of Dan, now."

"Wait- Daniel Gross?" The man from the list.

"Dan Gross." The wife said.

The boy brought a picture to show Alison. I came over to her to see the photo; the dad, mother and son were posing in front of a beach.

This connected the pieces; the tattoo was on Dan's shoulder.

"Alison." I pointed to it.

"I knew it." She said.

The wishbone was on Dan; it connected all of us together. A boy, a friend, a mother. But he didn't know I had one too. This was his tag; for his most prized possessions.

"Do you have any other pictures?' Alison asked.

The wife handed Alison another one, this time in front of a forest.

"Seems like a happy family." I looked up at the woman who was holding her child.

"Very." She smiled.

"Alison." An officer pointed closer to the picture.

"What is this?"

Alison looked to where the officer was pointing her hand; a cabin in the background, barely visible.

"It's a cabin we used to camp in."

"How many years ago?" Alison asked.

"Um- about 2?" The wife responded.

"Why did you stop?" I asked.

"Dan got busy." The mother responded.

"That's where she is." I looked at Alison.

"We need to go, Now!"

"What is going on?" The woman asked.

"We will explain later, come with me." One officer stayed behind gathering the woman and child together.

"I am taking you. Leave your car here."

We all ran outside to the car, excited and scared. Cade could be there right now, waiting for us. She wouldn't know her rescue was soon, seeing her face would be the best part.

"Get in." Alison said. The sirens of the car alarmed everyone in our way. Backup was following behind us as we made our way onto the highway.

"How far is it from here?" I asked.

"Not too far. He took me once."

It was about ten minutes into the car ride that the string loosened. "No!" I screamed.

"What, Nikki?" Alison asked.

"It's Cade. We aren't going to make it."

"Yes we will."

Her courage and optimism was appreciated, but her lie would soon become reality. It would hit me in the face and expose my weakest link- holding on.

"Hurry up, she doesn't have much time left."

Alison sped the car faster and I could feel my pulse rising.

"Nick." A voice in the back of me said.

"Cade. Hold on please."

"I don't have much time."

"No. you need to hold on."

"I want you to know- I forgive you, for everything."

What did Cade mean? This was too much.

"For the kiss. For trying."

"I am sorry."

"What is she saying Nikki?' Cameron asked.

"Don't be. I love you. Tell everyone I say goodbye- and love them."

"Just a little more."

She disappeared but the string didn't snap, that meant she was still going to try, and that was all I needed.

We stopped at a cabin in the woods. Alison took out her gun and all of us followed.

"Let's go. Stay behind me."

The door opened and the room was empty; no sign of life. Alison stepped in further and I turned my head seeing handcuffs on the ground. "Alison!" I pointed.

"Do not touch them." She ran over. "Move on, clear."

I stayed between Cameron and Ash. We followed a path down a couple of steps; I could hear rustling.

This was it.

I was ready to save my best friend. I was ready for the perfect ending. I was ready for the miracle.

Then snap. The string. What had kept me going; a sign that Cade was still alive all this time. Broken. Lost. In a body of souls, a lake of tears. Alison forced the door open and the shattered wood reminded me of the way I had felt. How the feeling of the wood snapping cut through my body and I felt like a vampire with the stake piercing my chest. I didn't care that we were here, I knew Cade was dead. They didn't know that.

The shots fired and he went down.

The bullets penetrated his body; but the evil of his soul remained.

There were not enough bullets in the world to end this monster's life.

He would always be the murderer who killed my best friend.

I saw Cade in the distance.

Her dismembered body looked fragile and bloody.

I was so close, and had let her down.

Her voice haunted my memory and her presence felt numb.

I had let everyone down.

The list of names didn't help save Cade. It killed her.

I'm told everything has a happy ending.

Cinderella, Beauty and the Beast, Snow White.

God.

I wish that was my life.

Well, that's about it.

All I needed to say.

That's all I know and all I remember.